A Time to Make Amends

(Book 6: An Irish Family Saga)

<u>by</u>

Jean Reinhardt

Historical Fiction

'This first light, though slight,
Is an intimation – a start,
And opens the closed-in feeling that
Lodges in the heart.'

'The Great Awakening' by Noel Sharkey

DEDICATION

To our grandchildren; Ethan, Robyn,
Lukas, Heidi and the little one expected to
arrive later in the year.

OTHER BOOKS BY THE AUTHOR

A Pocket Full of Shells (Book 1: An Irish Family Saga)

A Year of Broken Promises (Book 2: An Irish Family Saga)

A Turning of the Tide (Book 3: An Irish Family Saga)

A Legacy of Secrets (Book 4: An Irish Family Saga).

A Prodigal Return (Book 5: An Irish Family Saga)

The Finding Trilogy: a young adult medical thriller.

Book 1: Finding Kaden

Book 2: Finding Megan

Book 3: Finding Henry Brubaker

All books are in digital and paperback format on Amazon and Smashwords. They can also be ordered from The Book Depository and Createspace.

McGrother Family Tree

Pat and Annie McGrother: James's uncle and aunt.

Maggie: James's older widowed sister.

James McGrother married Mary Roarke (1845)
They had 5 children: Catherine, Thomas, Mary-Anne, Breege and Jamie.

Catherine married Patrick Gallagher (1866)
They had 3 children: Tom (Dr. Gilmore's Son), Maisie and Ellen.

Thomas's first wife was Jane (she died young).
They had 1 child: Eliza.
His second wife was Lily.
They had 1 child: Jeremiah (adopted).

Mary-Anne married Sergeant Broderick.
They had 1 child: George (Dr. Gilmore's son adopted by Mary-Anne).

Breege was single with no children.

Jamie married Annie.
They had two daughters.

CHAPTER ONE

Mary's eyes were drawn to the clock on the mantelpiece over the stove. It seemed to be staring back at her, its old face lined with tiny cracks. James reached up to where the latest news from their children in America had been stored carefully behind the old timepiece. Along with the four pages of cream notepaper, displaying their son's neat handwriting, the envelope contained letters from their grandchildren.

"Shall I read them again to you, Mary?" asked James, "I'll start with Eliza's."

The night closed in as the lantern threw its soft glow into the room. Maggie, who usually slept in the parlour, had retired for the evening leaving them alone. She had given up her bed when Mary was unwell so she wouldn't feel isolated in the bedroom at the back of the house. In the stillness of the night Maggie's rhythmic snoring filtered, in a strangely comforting way, through the adjoining door.

His wife having recently developed a fear of the dark, James made sure that should she awaken in the night, the lantern would always be lit to calm her anxious thoughts. In an effort to sleep, he would place the quilt over his head and with his eyes shielded from the light, slumber would eventually take over from a tiredness that never seemed to leave him. James found it ironic that the brightness keeping him awake was the only thing that could bring sleep to Mary.

Having read once more the cherished words from each of their grandchildren living in America, James carefully folded the letters before placing them into their shared envelope.

"Well, now, what do you make of our Eliza about to have a second wee one? That will be two great-grandchildren she's given us, Mary. Isn't she a grand girl, all the same – even if she *is* the wife of a Cork man? Sure we won't hold that against her, eh?"

Being used to his wife's silence, James continued the one-sided discussion about their grandchildren, asking questions he knew would not be answered. It had been a month since Mary suffered the stroke that paralyzed the left side of her face and she rarely tried to speak, embarrassed by the slurred words coming out of her mouth.

The sound of someone knocking on their door halted James in the middle of an old familiar tale he was relating to his wife.

"Come in, come in. We're all decent," he called out, smiling at Mary."

"Would you like me to sit with Ma for a while?" it was Mary-Anne, "The sergeant and George are doing some accounting and I thought it best to leave them get on with it. They were getting annoyed at me for correcting them."

Father and daughter laughed while Mary smiled inwardly.

"I think I've bored your ma enough for this evening. Haven't I, love? I daresay you'll be relieved to have a change of conversation."

"Where's Maggie? Out for a nice long walk, is she?"

James knew his daughter was being sarcastic but didn't rise to the bait, "She's having an early night, for a change."

Mary-Anne didn't reply but raised a caustic eyebrow.

"Right, so. I'll go see what the news is in Paddy Mac's," James kissed his wife's forehead. "I won't stay too long, Mary, nor drink too much either."

Alone with her mother, Mary-Anne busied herself sweeping a floor that didn't need cleaning.

"Did I tell you that George is making a grand name for himself at the shipping office, Ma?"

Mary had heard this on numerous occasions.

"I daresay he'll be put in charge when the day comes for his boss to retire," Mary-Anne chattered on as she made some tea.

Taking down the small stoneware invalid feeder from its place on the crockery shelf, Mary-Anne poured tea into it, not thinking to ask her mother whether or not she would like some.

"Here you go, Ma. Nice and hot, the way you like it."

Mary took the feeder from her daughter, holding its handle in her right hand, the left one weakened by the stroke.

"I wanted to buy you a bowl with a handle at the back, so that we could hold it for you. Did you know that, Ma? But the nurse said we were to get this one, with a handle you can hold for yourself. She told us we were not to mollycoddle you, can you believe that?" Mary-Anne tutted.

It was not easy for the young woman to stand by and watch her mother struggle to raise a trembling left hand to steady the feeder, but the family had been told by the hospital to encourage Mary to use her weakened arm and leg as much as possible. The long spout on the bowl ensured most of the liquid remained in her mouth but now and again a small dribble would escape to slide down the left side of her chin.

Mary-Anne chattered on, sharing whatever bit of gossip she had picked up that morning, automatically wiping away any drool of tea as quickly as it appeared. The unbroken flow of local news distracted both women from an affliction that had drastically changed their lives and although the conversation was one-sided, Mary was thankful for it.

Of all the family, James was the only one to look at his wife in the same way he had done for all the years they were together. Even Maggie, pragmatic as she was, found it hard to conceal the pity she felt for her sister-in-law. Mary could see it in her eyes but didn't blame her, had their situation being reversed she knew it would be impossible for her to hide her own sympathy.

Jamie and Annie's two little girls reacted as only children know how, innocently accepting their grandmother's state of health as something to adapt to. They were no longer allowed to sit on her knee and have their hair braided with the special brush they had previously been forbidden to touch.

Now the little girls delighted in taking turns gently stroking Mary's hair while admiring the red and yellow roses embroidered on the back of the brush. She enjoyed watching them disagree over whose turn it was to hold up the matching mirror and who should be doing the brushing. Mary never felt that she was being treated like an invalid as this was more like a game that she participated in, to the delight of her grandchildren.

When it came to adults it was a different matter, even James unconsciously made her feel helpless in his efforts to make her as comfortable as circumstances would allow. But Mary never once saw pity in his eyes, only concern, and she could tell the difference.

After a couple of hours filled with nothing to get excited about, the door opened and James entered the warm house. As she watched him remove his jacket, Mary hoped he had brought home more than the chilly breeze that followed him in from the street. She was hungry for any news he might have picked up in Paddy Mac's. Lately, she found men's gossip to be much more interesting than women's, or maybe it was because her husband now divulged news that he might not have shared with her before the stroke confined her to the house.

"Well, I'll be on my way," Mary-Anne squeezed her mother's good hand and kissed her cheek.

"Take your ma's heavy shawl," James held out a bundle of knitted black wool. "You'll freeze in the one you're wearing."

Once they were alone, James lowered the flame in the lantern and banked the stove before joining his wife in their warm bed. The familiar feel of her husband lying beside her, a long arm resting over her body, helped her to forget about her affliction as she waited patiently for him to share some news. Instead, shallow breathing told her that sleep had already overtaken him, no doubt helped by a pint or two.

Mary stroked the bearded cheek that had inched closer to her face and whispered a prayer of thanks for such a good husband, a lifelong companion. James had always said he hoped to be the one to go first and she knew he meant it. Now it looked as if he would have to face life without her, for Mary was sure that one morning he would wake up and she'd be gone. It was the reason why she found it so difficult to get to sleep at night.

The sound of muffled snoring from the other side of the parlour reached Mary's ears and she turned her head towards the door that led to her bedroom.

"I know, Maggie, I know. He will still have you," Mary said to herself. "Sure you'll outlive us all."

CHAPTER TWO

"How's that brother of mine, doing? I hear the fishing hasn't been so good of late, is that so?" asked Mary-Anne.

Annie filled a large wicker basket with her morning's baking, "He got himself a bit of work in Dromiskin, clearing away some overgrown hedges."

"Well, that's good to hear. With another wee one about to join the crew, you'll be needing every farthing you can get," Mary-Anne picked up a loaf of bread, still warm from the oven, and inhaled its mouth-watering aroma. "You are the only person I know who makes better bread than I do, Annie. I have a mind to increase the price I give you for it."

"Oh no, there is no need to do that. You've already been kind enough to give me the stove when you got your new one and it's made my life so much easier. You must thank Sergeant Broderick again for me. It was very good of him to put it in for us."

"Wasn't he the clever man, not telling Jamie where the stove had come from until it was in the fireplace and warming the house up?" added Mary-Anne. "He's another one drools over your food, Annie, and I imagine he's worried you'll be so busy with three children you might have to give up baking the bread and scones for us. If truth be told, I'm inclined to be a wee bit envious of your pastries, but the sergeant takes pride in his father's recipes and won't hear of me bringing anyone else's pies into the house."

A squabble broke out between two little girls behind Annie and she apologized to her visitor for the noise. The children could have been mistaken for twins, they were that close in age.

"I had best be off and leave you to your chores, that is if you get any done with those two rascals. You've your hands full with them already, Annie, how on earth will you manage a baby as well?" Mary-Anne tut-tutted as she walked away from her sister-in-law, not waiting for a response.

Annie turned to pick up her youngest daughter, reprimanding both girls as she did so. The family had recently moved into the small terraced cottage with its tiny attic bedroom. The larger ground floor room at the rear had been divided in two by Jamie and his father, with the landlord's permission, giving Annie a separate area to use as a scullery. This room led out to a long narrow plot, already dug over and soon to be planted. The rent had been almost twice what they were paying in their first home but Jamie had assured her the keeping of a pig and hens would help to offset the extra expense.

Taking her daughters by the hand, Annie brought them into the downstairs bedroom they shared with their parents and sat them down on a settle bed next to her own. She had inherited it from one of her grandmothers and it had plenty of room for two small children to share comfortably. They hadn't been living there long enough for the place to feel like home and Annie was not ready to have them sleep in another part of the house just yet.

"Let's all have a wee nap before your da gets home. Lie yourselves down there now and I'll tell ye a story that'll send the two of ye off into a land of butterflies and flowers."

CHAPTER THREE

As soon as he stepped through the door of Paddy Mac's the atmosphere changed, just for a few seconds, but James was acutely aware of it. The greetings he received were given with that little bit more warmth and by the time he reached the bar, having been patted on the back and shoulder so many times, Paddy Mac's son, Johnny, had his drink poured and waiting for him on the counter.

"Like walking on hot coals, was it, James? Those few steps from the door to here."

"They mean well, but you know yourself what it's like, having to face people after a long absence," James gulped down half his drink.

"You were in here two weeks ago, I would hardly call that a long absence," laughed Johnny.

"Is that all it was? It felt more like a month to me. Every day that we wait for Catherine to get here seems to have twice as many hours in it."

The barman gestured for James to lean over the counter and take a look at what stood on a shelf beneath it.

"I'm sorry, I haven't got anything to put in it this evening," James recognized the container that was used to collect money from Paddy Mac's clientele for anyone deemed in need of some financial assistance.

"This one is for you, James," Johnny put his hand up at the protest that was about to be let loose. "And don't be telling me you don't need it. We all know what it's like to be in your shoes and you've put a contribution in there yourself more times than I can count. I'll bring it over next week, before your daughter arrives and I daresay it will be full to the brim by then."

James sighed and raised his glass in salute to the younger man. "Do you miss America?" he asked, changing the subject.

As he poured a drink for another customer, Johnny thought for a moment before answering. "I would be lying to you if I said I didn't. It's a grand country, James, and a mighty place to find work if you're willing and able to do so."

"Aye, that's what my lot over there tell me in their letters. Before she left, Catherine promised to bring the children back for a visit and she kept her word, bless her heart, even though it was a struggle to find the fare. But it was only the girls that came with her, her son Tom was working. Did you know he's a printer now, and works with our Thomas for a newspaper? I haven't laid eyes on my grandson since he was a child and he's a grown man now. Do you remember our Catherine, Johnny?"

"How could I forget her, sure didn't my da send me out to run the legs off myself telling the neighbours of her arrival, the day she was born?"

James laughed at a memory that felt like it taken place only a few years before, yet was a lifetime ago for his daughter. "Your father was a fine man, Johnny. He's sorely missed.

Would you have come back from America if your mother hadn't needed someone here?"

"I was ready to come home, James, and that's the truth of it. I'm happy to have spent the last few years of my mother's life with her. Sure wasn't it a good thing I never stayed long enough in one place to settle down with a wife and children, as my brothers did?"

James reached into his pocket for some coins. "Speaking of wives, I'll just have one more before I go. I don't like to leave Mary for too long."

"The first drink was on the house, James, and no arguing."

"Thank you kindly, Johnny, you are your father's son, no doubt about it."

When the tankard had been emptied and placed back on the counter, James bade farewell to everyone and left as he had entered – his back patted all the way to the door.

Johnny looked across the room to where his wife was delivering bowls of soup to a table of hungry men. He congratulated himself on finding a good woman at such a late stage in his life. They would never have any children of their own to pass on the newly renovated Paddy Mac's to, but the business was providing them with a good living and the second floor he had built on overhead had given them a spacious home.

The hard years of labouring in America had certainly been worth it for Johnny. He had more money than even his wife knew about but a lot of it had been put aside for something other than home comforts.

CHAPTER FOUR

Catherine Gallagher took her son's hand to steady herself as she stepped from the horse drawn tram that brought them to the docks.

"You almost lost your bonnet up there Ma," laughed Tom. "Your cheeks are as rosy as a well ripened apple."

"On such a lovely day as this, it would have been a pity not to see the sights of Liverpool from the top deck, son. We were fortunate to have the weather on our side on the crossing over the Atlantic, I pray it will hold until we arrive in Dundalk."

Having purchased their tickets, mother and son made their way through the busy dockside to the pier where they were to board a steam packet to Dundalk. In the estuary where the Mersey raced towards the Irish Sea, enormous hoppers clanked noisily as they scooped out the channel, allowing the largest of vessels a clear passage, even at low tide. Fronting the docks were great big warehouses, storing a wide variety of commodities that had either been disembarked or awaited loading.

Once on board, it didn't take long to get settled into a chair on deck, Catherine and her son preferring to remain in the fresh, if somewhat chilly, air.

"Do you remember how long it took the last time you crossed from Liverpool to New York, Tom?"

"It didn't seem too long to us children, Ma. We had fun and games every day, if memory serves me right, but I imagine it was more daunting for you and Da."

Catherine sighed deeply, instinctively placing her hand on the lace trim at the neck of her blouse, where she knew a medal hung under her clothing.

"I was in such a state about the long crossing that your da bought me a St. Christopher to calm my nerves."

"Did it work, Ma?"

Tom's mother smiled and shook her head. "But don't you tell your da that. I let him think it helped, he had enough of his own worries weighing him down without adding mine to them."

"America is home to me now, Ma, and to the girls. It's where we've grown up. I can't imagine leaving it to return to live in Ireland as a bachelor, never mind if I had a wife and children to provide for. I can understand now, what a difficult decision it must have been for both of you to make," Tom lifted his mother's gloved hand and kissed it. "It was very thoughtful of you not to burden Da with your worries. You must be greatly relieved at how quickly these new ships can travel across the ocean today."

They both marvelled at how much faster the journey across the Atlantic had become, with the huge iron hulled liners making the crossing in as little as seven days, weather permitting.

The glances in their direction from young women strolling the deck brought a smile to Catherine's face, and she noted that Tom was oblivious to the attention. The only time her son acknowledged their presence was when two young ladies, walking slowly in front of them for the second time, came too close to his feet.

Tom didn't even look up, but continued in conversation with his mother as he pulled in his outstretched legs. Catherine had often worried that her husband Patrick might question the very obvious difference between their eldest son and his younger sisters. Tom's hair was black as coal and his long legs had given him a good three inches of height over his father.

As she looked into her son's eyes Catherine could see her own looking back at her and was grateful that he had not inherited the dark brown eyes of the man who had forced himself upon her, causing her to fall pregnant all those years before. For every one of Tom's twenty-five years Patrick had been a true father to her son and had loved him as much as he did their daughters. She hoped the day would never come when a question might be raised by either father or son on the very obvious disparity in appearance between Tom and his sisters.

Catherine had to bite her tongue on the rare occasion she had been tempted to share the heavy burden of her long held secret. It would be unfair to both men to inflict such a wound on their relationship, in an attempt to ease her conscience.

"You seem to be attracting quite a bit of attention from the young ladies on board, son," Catherine lowered her voice, "Those two that just passed by have been round twice already."

Tom automatically swept the deck with his eyes, laughing as he did.

"I hadn't noticed."

"I know you haven't, Tom. Is there someone back home who has already captured your heart?"

Tom leaned forward in his chair, resting his elbows on his knees. "There is indeed," he answered softly.

Two more young women passed by, so close their skirts bustled against Tom's feet.

"Do I know her?" Catherine's heart skipped a beat. This was a moment she had been anticipating and dreading. Her son was a very serious young man, devoted to his work at the newspaper and had never courted a girl before, to the best of her knowledge.

"I haven't told a soul. You mustn't tell anyone not even Da. Do I have your word?"

Catherine sighed deeply. "I'm very good at keeping secrets, Tom, but only tell me if you are quite sure about your feelings."

"When I am in a position to support a wife I plan on asking Mr. McIntyre for permission to call on Lottie.

The young man kept his eyes averted from his mother's gaze, not wanting to see what might be written in her expression. Although his employer, McIntyre, was a good friend of his uncle Thomas there were certain lines that should not be crossed and courting the boss's daughter was definitely one of them. That had been made clear to the staff the day before

Lottie began working for her father's newspaper.

"Does young Lottie know of your feelings towards her, Tom?"

"She does, Ma, and has been putting pressure on me to approach her father. We have been secretly passing notes to each other long before she ever came to work for him."

"Has she turned twenty-one yet?" asked Catherine.

"Three months from now and that is when I plan on speaking with her father."

"No, Tom. That is most definitely not the time to approach Mr. McIntyre. You must wait at least another six months to do that, else it will look as if you've been chasing his daughter behind his back."

Tom began to protest but his mother cut him short.

"And you must speak to your father of this as soon as you return home. Now, help me up out of this chair, son. I seem to have aged ten years in the last ten minutes, what will I be like when you make me a grandmother?"

The young man gave a hearty laugh as he stood to help his mother. "You might age a few more years when you stand up. The wind seems to be getting stronger."

Mother and son took their modest sized trunk and made their way to sit inside the saloon for the rest of the crossing. Had the day been warmer, Catherine would have quite happily dozed in her chair on the open deck. Tom joined some young men in a game of cards to pass the time, while Catherine claimed a corner seat, where she could lean back against the wall and take a nap.

As soon as land was in sight, Tom woke his mother, as she had instructed him to do, and they went out onto the deck. While most of the other women eventually retreated back into the relative warmth of the saloon, Catherine remained on deck. Facing the thin line of coast in the distance, she closed her eyes as a cold breeze washed over her face.

"Chailleann mé tú ró," she murmured.

Tom didn't understand the words his mother spoke and asked her what they meant.

"That wind you feel on your cheeks is Ireland blowing us kisses to welcome us home, son. I was telling her I missed her, too."

Tom nodded, placing an arm around his mother's shoulders. They stood silently watching an expanding band of green cut its way into the grey sea, as if the country was rushing through the water to meet them. The young man's eyes stung and watered as the wind grew stronger but he knew the tears rolling down his mother's cheeks were caused more by emotion than the weather, and he squeezed her arm in solidarity.

CHAPTER FIVE

The McGrothers were gathered together in the parlour of the family home, except for Mary, who had returned to sleeping in her own room and was too ill to be moved from her bed. George, Mary-Anne's adopted son, was also missing from the group, not yet home from work in Dundalk.

Over the previous twelve months, Jamie, the youngest of the McGrother children, had progressed to being on nodding terms with his older sister, Mary-Anne. This had relieved family gatherings of the awkwardness that would normally hang in the air whenever the two of them were in the same room.

"More tea, Jamie?" asked his wife.

"No thanks, Annie," he replied then lowered his voice to a whisper. "I could do with something a bit stronger, though."

"Save that for later. No doubt you'll be bringing your nephew for his first drink on Irish soil just as soon as you men can make good your escape."

Jamie tutted and smiled good-naturedly at his wife's jibe. "Go on with you, sure we all know that you women are delighted to see the back of us so ye can have a good old natter."

As Annie moved on to offer the tea to the rest of the room, Jamie's eyes went with her. He noticed his aunt Maggie seemed very subdued and wondered if her legs were playing up again. Some days she was unable to walk and spent most of her time sitting outside the door, weather permitting, snatching brief chats with anyone passing by.

He would like to have stood across the room beside his father but he was deep in conversation with Mary-Anne and her husband, Sergeant Broderick. Preferring to keep some distance between himself and his sister, Jamie made his way over to Maggie, who was entertaining his two little girls.

Picking the eldest one up from the chair next to her grandaunt, Jamie sat down and placed her on his lap, tickling her under the chin. This caught the attention of his younger daughter, who had been playing on the floor at Maggie's feet, and she jumped up, pretending to rescue her sister but seeking the same tickles from their father.

"Auntie Maggie has been telling us stories about you, Da," the older girl gasped in between the laughter.

"Then maybe I'm tickling the wrong person," James reached out to his aunt's side.

The girls held their breath as they watched their father's hand slowly make its way towards the layers of black fabric concealing Maggie's wide girth.

A sharp slap had him reeling it back and Jamie let out a mock howl, to the delight of his children. As he nursed his hand under his armpit Maggie laughed.

"My old legs may not move too well, young man, but the rest of me is as quick as ever it was."

"Did she hurt you, Da?" Jamie's youngest daughter pulled his hand out from beneath his jacket and kissed the back of it.

"She did, so you be careful to respect your elders or the same thing will happen to you. Now, the two of ye go over to the window and keep an eye out for our visitors. Let us know the minute you see the brake arrive, will you do that?"

Jamie was referring to the horse-drawn brake that Catherine and Tom would have boarded at Roden Place in the centre of Dundalk. Pulled by two horses, it could seat ten passengers and carry their luggage.

The girls were delighted to be given such an important task and climbed up on a bench that had been placed under the window. As Jamie watched them a moment of sadness overtook him and Maggie was quick to spot it.

"Are you thinking of the boys you lost, son?" Maggie was referring to two stillborn babies that Annie had delivered in the first few years of their marriage.

"You are quite the mind reader now, aren't you?" he replied.

"This one will be fine, you'll see. Look how healthy Annie is, I've never seen her look so well. I'm not saying it to ease your mind, either. This time it's a boy, I'm sure of it, and a healthy one at that."

Jamie squeezed his aunt's hand, "Maybe I'm not meant to have a son. I can live with that, Maggie, I would rather have another daughter than risk Annie losing a third baby. So I'm hoping it will be a girl."

A commotion at the window caught their attention and Jamie's daughters ran squealing into their father's arms, announcing the arrival of the brake from Dundalk. Maggie shouted above the excited children and told everyone to hush as she strained to see through the heavy lace curtains that Mary-Anne had bought for the occasion.

"Blasted nuisance these are. I can't see a thing. Your sister thinks we should all be as lordly as herself. Did you know she had young George white-wash the house the other day?"

"I was thinking it looked a bit fresher," to his surprise, Jamie found himself defending Mary-Anne. "She means well, Maggie. Let's not get ourselves into a bad mood with Catherine and Tom about to arrive any second."

Just as the words were out of his mouth, the door creaked open to reveal a smiling face. The room was so quiet the sound of the horses hooves could be heard fading into the distance as the brake moved on towards the heart of the village.

"I'm home," Catherine's voice quivered with emotion.

A huge cheer went up and as the door opened wider, a tall figure could be seen looming behind Catherine. Tom had to stoop low to follow his mother inside but stood back as she ran forward, straight into her father's arms. Hovering awkwardly just inside the door, he was very conscious of the fact that he was much taller than the other three men in the room.

It took Catherine a couple of minutes to compose herself before introducing Tom to his relatives. He was a young child when he last saw them but recognized his grandfather and grandaunt immediately. Mary-Anne's face took a bit longer to register and the man she stood next to was a complete stranger. Tom guessed he was Sergeant Broderick, married to his aunt, and was grateful that at least one man in the room was almost as tall as himself. Never before had his height bothered him as it did then, standing in his grandparents' house, being inspected by a gathering of people who were by all accounts strangers to him.

It didn't take long for the warm and loving welcome Tom received to put him at ease, especially the tight embrace his grandfather gave him after they had formally shaken hands.

"What on earth have you been feeding the boy, Catherine?" James pulled himself up to his full height as he asked the question.

The room filled with laughter and jokes about parents growing smaller as their children grew taller, and the difficulty of reprimanding a son who stands almost a foot higher than his mother.

"Not that I had much disciplining to do with Tom, he's been the best son any woman could have asked for," Catherine beamed with pride.

"She always made me sit down before chastising me, didn't you, Ma?" added Tom.

"Well, you come over here now, young man, and sit by me and I'll come up with something to berate you over," Maggie was patting the empty chair next to her. "I expect you're anxious to see your mother, Catherine. Why don't you bring her in a nice sup of tea, love? James, go on in with her, it will be a shock at first for the poor girl."

The good cheer and warmth was immediately sucked out of the room and

Maggie had no regret about that. She could picture her sister-in-law lying in her sick-bed in the small back room, listening to the cheerful home-coming but unable to participate, and did not want to prolong her isolation a moment longer.

Mary-Anne had quickly filled the invalid bowl with sweetened tea and handed it to her father as he escorted Catherine towards the back of the house. No words were spoken and Tom's heartbeat quickened as he watched his mother leave the room, knowing she would soon be calling him in to join her.

CHAPTER SIX

A welcome silence had descended on the room and nobody seemed inclined to break it. Slowly, the sound of the street below crept in to fill the space and Lily sighed contentedly as she leaned back into her chair.

"That was a lovely surprise, thank you, Patrick. It's not often I have no cooking to do on a Sunday."

"It was our Maisie's idea, Lily, she's been looking after us almost as well as her mother does, in spite of the long hours she puts in at the factory. I thought she was going to burst with pride with all the praise you two were giving her over the food," Patrick replied. "I didn't get a chance to thank you properly for giving Catherine the price of the fare over to Ireland, Thomas, it meant a lot to her. I'm afraid there was no way of us raising the funds ourselves at such short notice and our Tom used up all of his savings on his own ticket."

Thomas was very quiet and it was Lily who spoke next.

"We could have borrowed the price of the fare, Patrick, but it's been less than a year since Thomas and Jeremiah's last trip over. It was only fair that Catherine should have the chance to see her mother before . . . before . . ."

"Maisie's young man, Sean Dillon, seems a nice enough fellow," Thomas piped up. "I gave him the protective uncle stare, just to make sure he knows to behave himself with my niece."

Lily poked her husband in the ribs, grateful that he had changed the subject.

"I saw it, and if he still wants to court Maisie after that, then he's a brave man," she said.

Patrick laughed and added that it was the same stare he had given the young suitor when he asked for permission to call on Maisie. Catherine had been prepared for the occasion, as a mother usually is, and took it all in her stride – but not Patrick. His own attempt to gain permission from James McGrother to court his daughter had not gone well and it had taken his father-in-law quite a few years to finally offer a true hand of friendship. Unfortunately, it wasn't until Patrick and Catherine were leaving to make a new life in America with their children, that James removed the barrier that had caused so much tension between them.

"You've gone very quiet, Patrick. You're not worried about Maisie going to the theatre with her young man, are you?" asked Thomas.

"Sure they've enough chaperones with them," said Lily. "Our Jeremiah and your Ellen will keep them on their toes. Catherine told me she overheard Maisie telling her sister to stop drooling over Sean and to go out and find a man of her own."

"Ah sure, I know I've no need to be anxious," Patrick replied. "I was remembering how long it took your own father to accept me into the family, Thomas."

"Oh, for goodness sake, what are we doing getting all maudlin on such a fine day? Why don't we spend the afternoon at the park," Lily rose from her chair and gave the men a cheerful smile.

"You're absolutely right, my dear," said Thomas. "Come on, Patrick. It's not often we are free of the children on a Sunday afternoon."

"I have something to show you before we go, Thomas," Patrick took an envelope down from behind a clock on the mantelpiece. "It came for our Tom on Friday. Looks very official to me, I'm not sure if I should leave it till he's back to find out what's inside. Maybe it's something important that needs replying to sooner. What do you think?"

Thomas inspected the envelope, "It's from a lawyer, here in New York. Do you think Tom is expecting such a letter?"

Patrick shook his head, "He would have told us about it, knowing it might arrive in his absence."

Handing the unopened envelope back to his brother-in-law, Thomas suggested he leave it that way for the present.

"Why not have that walk while you ponder over it, Patrick? We don't want to disappoint Lily, do we?"

After taking a horse-drawn streetcar to Central Park the trio strolled along the broad avenue of The Mall, mingling with the city's afternoon strollers. Lily linked her husband's arm as she studied the faces of the women sitting on the benches on either side of them, not wanting to miss saluting a neighbour or a friend. Thomas on the other hand, had spotted a small crowd of people ahead and picked up the pace a little, the journalist in him not wanting to miss anything, however insignificant. If a radical speech was taking place it would not be too long before the police made their appearance.

A loud voice boomed and brought them to an abrupt standstill, the owner of which was a middle-aged man in a well-worn suit. Most of the people listening to him were women and he looked as if he would burst into tears at any moment.

They stood listening to his heartfelt speech for a while and Lily feared she would be reduced to tears should they stay for much longer. Some of the women around her were already dabbing their cheeks. The poor man had been a slave to drink and when his business failed because of it, he lost his house and possessions. But it was the loss of his family that finally made him come to his senses. His wife, finding herself at the end of her tether, took their children and went back to live with her parents, two hundred miles away.

Lily pulled at the arms of the two men and gave them a beseeching look.

"I shall be crying my eyes out soon, if we don't move on," she said.

They continued their stroll, leaving behind the contrite speaker as he went on to denounce the demon drink and advocate the gift of temperance.

"Do you ever think about being more involved in social matters yourself, Patrick?"

asked Thomas. "I'm sure Catherine has softened in her attitude to your political beliefs by now. In fact it's been a long time since I heard her berate you for not going to Mass with the family."

"Do not let my wife's silence on both of those subjects fool you. I still get that look from her on a Sunday morning. Her face says enough to me without a word having to leave her lips. I made Catherine a promise when we came to America. I swore to her that I would steer clear of politics and be moderate in my drinking habits and, for most of the time, I have kept to my word."

"And Catherine very much appreciates it, Patrick. On more than a few occasions she has told me how fortunate she is to have such a good sober husband and father for her children," Lily was reminding Patrick of his wife's devotion to him.

Thomas noticed his brother-in-law's obvious discomfort and tried to change the subject.

"The demon drink can wreak havoc on families caught in its trap. We see evidence of that all around us, do we not?" Thomas gestured back to the speaker.

"It's poverty that is the demon, not the drink. Do you think a man feels at ease watching his children go to bed cold and hungry, in a corner of the one damp and dismal room his meagre wage allows him to rent? How is he to look his wife in the eye day after day, unable to provide a decent home and food for his family?"

"Why, Patrick, you sound as if you've given this a lot of thought. Those words have the makings of a good speech. Are they your own?" asked Thomas.

The two men stared at each other and Lily wished she had kept silent about Patrick's sobriety.

"Do you think that because I cannot read or write I'm incapable of forming opinions?"

"Not at all, Patrick. I am well aware of how opinionated you can be," Thomas had lowered his voice a fraction below his brother-in-law's tone. "But you also have a good memory when it comes to relaying speeches you have paid close attention to. I merely thought that your words came from one of those. If not, then you should think on expanding them into something that can be delivered in a setting such as this," Thomas swept his arm in a wide circle.

Even Lily was unsure of her husband's tone. She knew that he was not mocking Patrick but detected a trace of antagonism in his voice.

"We had best be getting home, gentlemen, our children will be thinking we have abandoned them," she said.

Both men turned to Lily but Patrick could not look her in the eye. This was unusual behaviour for him and made her uncomfortable in his presence.

"Yes, I suppose we should get back before the children arrive home. There's that letter that needs to be read, Patrick. That is, if you still want to open it. Or would you prefer Maisie read it?" asked Thomas.

Patrick shook his head, "I'm not sure I should open it before having a word with Tom first. I might send a telegram and let him decide. Sure he'll be home in a couple of weeks anyway."

"I think that's a wise decision, Patrick," Lily had a strange foreboding about the content of the legal envelope. "We must quicken our step to keep warm. There's a bit of a chill in the air and I'll be happy when we are all back at your place in front of a warm stove."

The men agreed with her and she linked her arms through theirs, almost running to keep up with them, relieved that the tension between her husband and his brother-in-law had disappeared as quickly as it had arrived.

CHAPTER SEVEN

Catherine was surprised to find her mother's eyes closed when she entered the room and turned to look back at her father. James, who had insisted she go in before him, waved her on and pointed to a rocking chair next to the bed.

The cushion she sat on was deep and felt as good as a mattress and Catherine settled into its well indented shape. She searched every inch of her mother's face for a sign of illness or any pain but if anything, Mary McGrother looked exactly the same as the last time her daughter had set eyes on her, eight years earlier.

It wasn't that the family in America were too busy to visit more often but the cost was something that put such trips beyond their means. Many of their Irish friends had never been back at all, even after twenty or thirty years, and few of them had received visits from parents. Any siblings or relatives who did make the journey across the Atlantic usually travelled on a one way ticket, intent on emigrating and hopeful of finding enough work to make a good life for themselves.

"She looks so peaceful, Da. She's not in any pain is she?" whispered Catherine.

James looked sadly at his wife's relaxed face. How could he tell his daughter of her mother's tormented dreams that left her in fear of the dark? She would soon see for herself, his wife's bitter frustration at not being able to speak. The second stroke she suffered, just a week before Catherine's arrival, had taken away from Mary any chance she may have had of uttering another coherent word. She had given up trying, embarrassed by the sound of the grunts that came through her slack lips.

As he reached out for his daughter's hand Mary's eyes began to flicker open and James prepared himself for the shock that Catherine would experience at the sight of her poor mother trying to force a smile. Mary had been practising for two days but her expression resembled more of a painful grimace than the beautiful warm smile that had won James's heart as a young boy.

He needn't have worried about Catherine's response. As soon as Mary opened her good eye, the beam of delight at seeing her eldest child was clearly visible and an immediate connection was made between the two women. It was as if Catherine was completely unaware of any disfigurement on her mother's face and James knew he wasn't needed at that moment.

"I'll leave you two alone for a wee while," he kissed Mary on the forehead while lightly squeezing his daughter's hand.

As soon as the door closed behind her, Catherine put her head on Mary's breast and allowed the tears she had hidden from her father to flow freely. This was her mother, a woman well used to seeing her children weeping. Even in sickness, she had the ability to give comfort and Mary squeezed Catherine's hand with the one she still had power in, allowing some of her own tears to escape.

Once she had regained her composure, Catherine raised her head and kissed her mother on the cheek that sagged, then moved her lips to the half-closed eye.

"Do you want some of that tea, Ma, before it goes cold on you?"

Mary nodded her head and as Catherine leaned across to fetch the invalid bowl the faintest hint of perfume filled the air around them.

'*She has the scent of an American woman about her,*' thought Mary, '*But she is still my wee girl.*'

Raising her mother's head to make it easier to swallow, Catherine carefully held the bowl to Mary's lips and watched her take a long drink. It reminded her of a time when she was a young girl and found herself in a similar situation.

"I'll sit this back here on the table, Ma. If you want another sup let me know. Or are you not able to speak to me?"

Catherine saw the anxiety enter Mary's eyes and assured her that there was no need to worry about communicating with her.

"Just point your finger towards the bowl and I'll know what you want, Ma. That's easy enough now, isn't it?"

She took something from her bag and smiled at it before showing it to her mother.

"I brought you a present. Look, we went to a photographer's studio and had a family portrait done."

Mary looked at the beautiful family in the ornate, silver-over-copper frame and recognized her grandchildren straight away. She was shocked at how much of a man her grandson had become but the girls hadn't changed too much since their last visit to Ireland.

Catherine chatted away, giving her mother the news of the family back in New York. She took another photograph in a matching frame and placed it on the bedside table beside the first one. There were three people in this one.

"Doesn't our Thomas look like a proper lord of the manor, with his fancy clothes? Himself and Lily are doing very well, Ma, and young Jeremiah is a right little scholar. Says he wants to be a doctor. He never stops talking about you and Da, ever since his trip over last year. Thomas is planning another visit soon, Ma. You'll like that, won't you?" Catherine wiped a dribble from the corner of her mother's mouth.

The simple action reminded Mary of the time when she was pregnant with her youngest daughter, Breege, and trapped in a state of depression. Catherine, being the eldest and only ten years old, fed her mother and combed her hair. Mary was wondering if her daughter remembered this when Catherine's voice broke into her thoughts.

"This brings me back, Ma. Do you remember how I used to do this for you when you were having a hard time on our Breege?"

Half of Mary's face twisted into a smile and Catherine instinctively knew her mother had been recalling the same memory.

"Well, now that I'm older I'm a wee bit more patient, so there's no need to feel you have to gulp your tea down quickly. Sip it slowly like you've always done. I've never known anyone can make a cup of tea last as long as you, Ma."

Catherine ran her fingers through the hair at the top of her mother's head. She noted how much greyer it had become in the years since she had last laid eyes on it and assumed a lot of that was due to the strokes she had suffered.

"I'll wash your hair whenever you feel up to it, Ma. It's still as pretty as ever, even with all those silver strands running through it. I think I might even be envious of you," Catherine produced a comb from her bag. "Here, let me just tidy away those stray bits and get you ready to meet your grandson. He's been so eager to see you, it's all he talked about on the journey over."

Although she was happy to meet her grandson after all those years apart, the young man Mary had seen in the photograph would be a stranger to her and she was not sure how she felt about seeing his reaction to her afflictions.

"I'll go and fetch him, Ma. I haven't tired you out with all my chatter, have I?"

Without waiting to see what her mother's response to her question was, Catherine stood up to leave the room and felt a tug on her skirt.

"Whatever is the matter? Do you not feel up to meeting our Tom? Would you rather leave it till after you've had a wee nap?"

Mary nodded her head and gave Catherine the half-smile that had already become a familiar expression to her daughter in their short time together.

"All right so, Ma. You close your eyes now and rest yourself. Our Tom can see you this evening, I'm sure Da is anxious to bring him up to Paddy Mac's and show the neighbours what a fine young man his grandson has turned out to be."

Left alone in her bedroom, Mary sighed deeply and turned her head in the direction of the two photographs sitting on the bedside table. She gazed at the young man standing behind his father and mother, his two sisters on each side of him. How different he looked from the young child that left for America two decades ago. Mary was relieved that Catherine could read her so well. She knew that later in the evening, when the last bit of daylight had faded and with only a small flame in the lantern to illuminate the room, she would not find it so disconcerting to show herself to her grandson.

CHAPTER EIGHT

Lily nestled into the padded back of her armchair and stared at the flames of an open fire. A spark flew out, landing on Thomas's shoe, and they both leaned forward at the same time to brush it off. The book he was reading fell with a soft thump onto the floor and Lily picked it up, examining the cover before handing it over.

"What is it about, Thomas?"

"I borrowed it from William McIntyre. He knows the author, Jacob Riis, quite well. I've met him myself on occasion. He strikes me as a caring enough fellow, but I cannot make up my mind as to whether or not he is genuine in his sentiment."

"Sentiment about what?"

Thomas opened the book and pointed out a photograph of a thin, ragged child to his wife, "What do you make of someone who devotes so much time to recording such distressing images, Lily?"

"I've seen some of those photographs before. Do they not make the well-off more aware of the plight of those less fortunate than themselves? Surely that can only be a good thing."

"It depends on the motive, Lily. There money to be made in making a public display of such poverty, people are curious about how the other half lives. Hence the title of this book."

As Lily could not read very well, her husband drew his finger under the lettering on the front cover of the book, repeating the words *How the Other Half Lives.*

In the mid 1800's in England, in the city of London, the wealthy had taken to visiting impoverished tenements on guided slum tours, often referred to as *slumming.* This form of tourism also took place in the Bowery and Five Points area of New York but on a much smaller scale.

"Well, if it causes the wealthy to share some of their riches with the poor, what harm is there in it?" asked Lily.

Thomas stared into the flames, thinking about his own past and the loss of his first wife at such a young age. Her untimely death, due to a life of unhealthy working conditions in a cotton mill, had resulted in their daughter growing up without a mother, raised by his parents in Ireland. Although he did not regret his decision to leave Eliza with her grandparents while he took up an offer of work in America, Thomas felt remorse at missing out on so much of her childhood. Now she was a grown woman, living less than two hundred miles from them with a husband and children of her own, yet they hardly saw each other.

"Thomas?"

"I'm sorry, Lily. I'm not very good company this evening. Did you notice a coolness between myself and Patrick while we were at the park?"

Lily admitted she had noticed an obvious strain between the two men but thought better of questioning him about it.

"Now that you've mentioned it, my love, would you like to tell me why you feel that way? Have you two been quarrelling over something?" she asked.

Remembering a train journey from Philadelphia to New York a decade before, when he almost came to blows with his brother-in-law, Thomas wondered how much of that account he should reveal to Lily. He was sure that Patrick had never spoken a word of what he had done to Catherine, the taking of a man's life was not an easy thing to tell one's wife about.

"There has been an uneasiness between Patrick and myself for the past ten years, ever since we rescued young Petey Halpin from that vile place in Pennsylvania. Do you remember how often you mentioned it to me upon our return?"

"I thought you had put whatever differences you had behind you. What has changed, Thomas?"

"I saw a different side to Patrick at the time and I let him know. I'm not sure he has truly forgiven me for speaking my mind," Thomas turned the book over in his hands. "This man, Jacob Riis, whatever his motives may be, at least he is being true to himself. Patrick has been avoiding the life he really wants to live, ever since he came to America. Did you know that the quarrymen asked him to be their spokesman some years back and he declined?"

Lily shook her head, the Patrick she knew was not the type to put himself in the spotlight. She would never have taken him for a leader, in fact, he didn't seem to be a follower either. It was Lily's belief that Patrick Gallagher was a mild tempered family man who had no other ambition in life but to keep his family healthy and happy and to see his children thrive.

"He refuses to go to Church, does he not? Nothing Catherine says has changed his mind on that. How is he not being true to himself? What are you trying to tell me, Thomas?"

"Now that the children are almost grown, I can see a change coming about in Patrick. Those impassioned words you heard him utter today are but a small fraction of what he carries in his heart, Lily."

Thomas saw a look of consternation appear on his wife's face and felt bad about ending their evening on an unpleasant note.

"Let's not dwell on this any longer, my love. Look how fortunate we have been, we have a nice flat in a good area of the city with an indoor toilet, heating, and piped hot water to boot. Is that not enough to bring the smile back to your lovely face?"

"It is. It really is, Thomas. But I must ask you one more question and I want an honest answer. Do you wish that you could be more of a participant in radical activities, like those that you write about in your newspaper reports?"

"No, Lily. I have never been inclined to throw stones at injustice or shout out grievances against those who inflict them. The

47

written word is my chosen weapon and my main concern is to report and record these events. I try to keep my convictions and feelings separate from what I write. The readers will come to their own conclusions and make their own judgements."

"But what about Patrick? Why do you say he is not being true to himself?" asked Lily.

Thomas stood and held a hand out to his wife.

"Come now, Lily, you said only one more question, did you not? Let's be getting to our bed, it's been a long day."

Lily took his hand and smiled as she rose out of her chair. The day had indeed been long and tiring for her, and she determined to put any concerns about her brother-in-law out of her mind.

******

After turning the envelope over and over in his hands, Patrick placed it back where it had been safely stored behind the clock. He would get Maisie to send a telegraph to his son the next morning but he knew what the answer would be. Curiosity would get the better of young Tom and he would want to know what it was all about. Even his sisters were anxious to read the contents of such an important looking envelope but it was not right to read another man's correspondence without his permission, so Patrick would wait patiently for his son's answer from Ireland.

CHAPTER NINE

Tom's mouth went dry when he saw his mother come out from the bedroom and close the door behind her. He had been anxiously waiting for her to fetch him in to meet his ailing grandmother.

"I fear I may have worn out my poor mother," Catherine turned to her father, "Maybe yourself and Jamie would like to take our Tom down to Paddy Mac's for a wee drink before supper. Oh, and you, too, of course Sergeant Broderick."

It was a very relieved young man that left the McGrother household with his male relatives. Tom knew that eventually he would have to face his ailing grandmother but fortified by a little alcohol, he would find the situation a lot easier to cope with. He knew how different he would appear to her, as if he were a stranger. Tom hoped the photograph his mother had brought with them would take away some of the shock his grandmother would experience upon seeing a grown man, and a very tall one at that, in place of the little grandson she had kissed goodbye all those years before.

Annie went home with her children shortly after the men departed and the house seemed to sigh in the quietness.

"Help me up girls. My poor old legs need a good stretch."

"You don't intend on taking a walk, Aunt Maggie, do you?"

"And what of it, if I did, Mary-Anne?"

The look of disapproval on the younger woman's face took Catherine by surprise, not many people stood up to her father's sister so openly.

"I'll take you out for a wee stroll if you like, Aunt Maggie," offered Catherine.

Mary-Anne redirected her frown towards her sister and it was obvious a row was about to erupt.

"Heaven's above, the two of ye are as quick to disagree as ever. It's like being with a pair of ten year-olds, scowling at one another," Maggie tutted and shook her head. "I have no intention of putting my nose outside that door. I mean to lie flat on my bed and stretch out my poor old limbs while I take a nap."

The sisters took in the expression on each other's faces, then broke out in quiet laughter, conscious of their sleeping mother in the back room. They helped Maggie to her bed in the corner of the parlour and it wasn't long before her low snores came from behind the curtain draped around her.

"At last, she's off," said Mary-Anne. "We might have a bit of peace while we sup our tea."

"How does our poor father manage at all? Two sick women in the house and him having to bring in a wage at the same time?" wondered Catherine.

"He has plenty of help between myself and Annie," Mary-Anne replied sharply.

"Oh I didn't mean to offend you, I'm sure both of you are very capable, but you have families of your own to care for. You cannot be here all the time, surely?"

"And what do you suggest we do, Catherine? Send our mother and our aunt to the workhouse?"

Catherine sighed at her sister's old habit of putting words into her mouth. She had promised herself to be patient and bite her tongue should Mary-Anne try to rise her.

"I was thinking that I might stay on after . . . should Ma . . ."

"I'm sure Da would be very happy to have you do that, Catherine," Mary-Anne replied quickly, preventing her sister from speaking the words neither of them wanted to hear.

She looked at the clock on the mantelpiece, its face stained the colour of tea from decades of smoke rising up from the stove below.

"Our George should have been home by now. He did tell me he had to stay after work for an important test he must take, but he is never this late."

"I cannot wait to see him. George was only a wee boy the last time I laid eyes on him and now he a young man. He's a credit to you, Mary-Anne. And to your husband," said Catherine.

A soft tap on the door interrupted the conversation and when Mary-Anne opened it a young boy stood on the step and whispered a message from George. She nodded and patted the child's tuft of dirty blonde hair before closing the door.

"Well, that must be the quietest child in the parish," said Catherine, "He barely spoke."

"George told him not to make any noise for fear of disturbing his grandmother. He's with the men in Paddy Mac's – they met him on the way there. He'll be starving by the time he gets home, that boy has the appetite of a horse."

"I can help you with the meal, Mary-Anne."

"There's not much to do, really. Most of it is cooked already but you could take one of those potatoes out of its skin and mix it through this wee pot of broth I have here for Ma."

As the two women worked at their tasks they made light conversation, speaking of their children and husbands but Catherine avoided talking about the one person weighing heavily on her mind – their mother. Not once in any of the letters to America had anyone mentioned exactly how serious her condition was, but there had been an unmistakeable sense of urgency about them. Even so, Catherine was still shocked by the sight that met her eyes upon entering her parents' bedroom.

Mary-Anne had just made a fresh pot of tea when a voice called out to her from the corner of the room.

"I'll bring a cup over to you, Aunt Maggie, supper is almost ready," said Catherine.

"Thank you, my dear. My legs are still asleep, I think I might have my supper here in my bed as well. Your hard-hearted sister would have me crawl over to the table on my hands and knees."

Mary-Anne rolled her eyes but held her tongue. She did not want to rise to her aunt's bait and have the men come home in the middle of an argument.

"Now, now, Aunt Maggie. A wee bit of exercise won't do you any harm but if you cannot wake up those legs of yours then I'm sure Mary-Anne has no objection to you eating your supper in bed," Catherine looked at her sister.

"Of course I don't. Why, you can even spoon-feed her if you like, then her arms can go to sleep, too," Mary-Anne could no longer hold back.

"See how she speaks to me, Catherine," Maggie whispered. "If it weren't for your father, she would have me in the workhouse by now."

"I heard that. I've already made enquiries but they know what trouble you can be and refused to have you."

"Mary-Anne, don't make light of such a thing," said Catherine. "She's only jesting, Aunt Maggie."

"Ah, I should have stayed asleep and kept my mouth shut," the old woman groaned.

"Your mouth is never shut – awake or asleep. Did you not hear the snores of her, Catherine? Only a mouth as wide as Dundalk Bay could produce a noise like that."

Before Maggie had a chance to respond the door opened and James stepped into the house, enquiring if Mary had rung for help. He had fixed a small bell to a string, which looped through a hook in the ceiling above the bed. The string was tied around a wooden dowel that lay near Mary's good hand and all she had to do was pull it whenever she wanted to summon one of them.

As the men spilled into the cottage the sound of muffled laughter could be heard outside. Catherine recognized her son's voice and smiled when she saw how low he had to bow his head and shoulders as he came through the doorway. The last person to appear was George, Mary-Anne's adopted son, and he, too, had to duck quite low as he entered the house. When he straightened himself up and stood beside his cousin there was no mistaking the resemblance and yet, as far as the family knew, there was no blood relationship between them.

Catherine's head spun, the two of them looked like brothers, and she knew straight away who had fathered George. Dragging her eyes from the young men to where her sister stood across the parlour, she saw a look of surprise on Mary-Anne's face and felt an awkwardness fill the room.

The ringing of a bell caught everyone's attention but James was first to react. Catherine told him about the bowl of food she had prepared for her mother and he collected it on his way to the bedroom door, instructing his family to begin their meal without him. As he disappeared into the dimly lit room a low hum of conversation began. Mary-Anne introduced her son to Catherine, as she sat him and the rest of the family around the table. She was careful not to place him near Tom in case someone might remark on their uncanny likeness.

There was a slight strain in the air as Catherine answered even more questions about New York – the cost of living and a regular wage being top of the list. She was happy to have the diversion, as every time she looked up from her plate she caught site of her son at one end of the table or her nephew at the other, both of whom seemed oblivious to their unsettling resemblance.

While his supper was keeping warm on the top of the stove, James fed Mary in the quietness of their room. He gave her the news from the parish he had picked up in Paddy Mac's and told her how proud he had been to stand next to their fine tall grandson, who was head and shoulders above all the other men there. A sudden urge swept over James to tell his wife of their eldest daughter's terrible secret, which he had promised never to reveal to anyone.

In her fragile state, it would be too distressing for Mary to be told that Catherine had been raped by a stranger, then married Patrick when she found out she was pregnant. That was not something a sick mother should hear and James decided to spare her the pain. But Mary was bound to see the likeness between the cousins and that would raise a question he knew she would want an answer to.

It was now obvious to James that Mary-Anne did not adopt her son but had given birth to him herself. The same question must have entered the heads of Jamie and Sergeant Broderick when they encountered George on the road earlier on their way to Paddy Mac's, and saw him next to Tom.

Lost in his unsettling thoughts, James felt a light squeeze of his hand and realized that Mary was trying to ask him something. Even if it took him a while, he always understood her needs and this time it was clear that she wanted to see her eldest grandson.

"I'll just turn up the lantern, my love."

Mary became agitated as the room brightened and James instinctively knew what was wrong and brought the flame down.

"Don't fret so, Mary. I shall leave just enough light to prevent young Tom from stumbling and landing on top of you in the bed."

CHAPTER TEN

When Patrick arrived home from the quarry, hungry and tired, he found Maisie busy at the sink.

"There's talk of another strike," he announced.

"When is there not a strike taking place somewhere? Sit yourself down first and eat your supper, Da. You can wash later," Maisie replied.

"Your Ma would kill me if she knew I sat at her table in my dusty old work clothes."

"Sure, it will be our little secret, Da."

While her father ate, Maisie sipped her tea and pondered over the unopened enveloped addressed to her brother. She had sent a telegram to him in Ireland and received the news that day to go ahead and read the contents.

"Ellen was here today when a telegram arrived from Tom. He says we're to read that letter and let him know what it's about," Maisie took a slip of paper from her pocket. "I've been waiting for you to get home so we could open it together. Shall I do it now?"

"Where is Ellen, surely not in bed at this early hour?"

Patrick had a terrible feeling in the pit of his stomach about the mysterious letter and wanted to delay the reading of it for as long as possible.

"Do you not recall her telling you this morning that she would be staying overnight at Thomas and Lily's to help Jeremiah with his schoolwork?"

"Oh yes, I had forgotten. Your sister has the makings of a fine teacher."

"The letter, Da? Shall I open it now? Are you not curious as to what it might be about?"

Patrick sighed and agreed that the contents of the envelope had been playing on his mind ever since its arrival, but he didn't reveal the fact that he had an uneasy foreboding about it.

Maisie carefully opened the envelope as if it was made of eggshells and might fall apart in her hands. As she read out slowly from the neat script Patrick hung on every sentence.

"Read it again, love. Are you sure that's what it says?"

"Yes, Da. I was careful to pronounce every word correctly. *Substantial* means a large amount. Why would a stranger leave our Tom so much money in his will?"

"Why indeed, Maisie. Why indeed. Tom needs to be told about this tomorrow."

Patrick went very quiet, the feeling in his stomach intensifying, and Maisie saw his discomfort.

"Is this not grcat news for Tom? Why do you have such a pained expression on your face, Da? Surely you must be happy for him."

Patrick slowly rose from the table, something was pulling him into his past but he couldn't quite put a finger on it. The name of his son's benefactor echoed in his head until a face eventually appeared, as clear as day. At first he thought it was Tom but the man was much older. When the full realization of what his subconscious was trying to tell him finally hit home, Patrick's knees went week and he collapsed onto his chair.

Maisie raced around the table and used her apron to fan him.

"Whatever ails you, Da? You've gone as white as a sheet."

The concern in his daughter's voice brought Patrick to his senses and he forced a weak smile. This was enough to reassure Maisie and she helped him move from the table to his armchair near the stove.

"I'm fine, girl. Don't be fretting over your old da. Whatever it is that Tom has inherited, I hope he spends it wisely."

"Of course he will. That's not something you need worry about."

Glancing at the clock where the letter had once stood, Maisie remarked on the time and reminded her father that Sean would be calling to collect her very shortly.

"Shall I ask him to stay here, Da? We were only going to see a play. It will still be on at the weekend."

Patrick assured his daughter that he would be fine on his own and was looking forward to having the place to himself. When Sean arrived it didn't help that he remarked on how tired her father looked and Maisie refused to leave the apartment. It took a lot of persuading by Patrick to make the young couple go out for the evening. It was only when he promised to take a walk and call on his brother-in-law that she relented and put on her coat.

"The fresh air will do me good, Maisie, and clear the quarry out of my lungs. Now, you two young people go off and enjoy your evening together."

Patrick had to physically push both of them through the door and into the hallway.

"Go on, now, off with ye, and give me a bit of peace," he shooed them away as if they were a couple of annoying hens.

Their laughter echoed back towards him even after they had turned a corner in the hallway and were no longer visible. Patrick took his hat and coat from behind the door and left his warm apartment to keep the promise he had made to his daughter. As he put his son's letter into his pocket, he wondered what Thomas and Lily might make of it. He would study their reaction carefully to see how they responded to the news of his son's good fortune. When he explained to them who that benefactor was, would they come to the same conclusion as himself? More importantly for Patrick, would they be honest with him if they did?

CHAPTER ELEVEN

"The house is nice and quiet now that everyone has left. They told me to wish you a good night from them."

Tom held his grandmother's hands and looked deep into her eyes. He was barely able to hide his shock at how much she had aged compared to his grandfather. The last stroke she had would have killed a large man, never mind the frail little woman who lay before him. Tom knew she had held on for their arrival and prayed that her strength would last long enough for his mother to spend more time with her.

"I have a secret to share with you, Mamó. Ma said I should call you that, she said it would be more pleasing to you than *Grandmother* and I much prefer it myself."

Mary slowly nodded her head and waited to hear what news was about to be imparted.

"You must not tell anyone, Mamó. I only revealed it to Ma when we set out from Liverpool," Tom gave a quick glance back towards the bedroom door. "Nobody else knows about it. Not yet, anyways."

Mary was examining every inch of her grandson's face, his resemblance to George unmistakeable, even in the dim light. His words barely registered as her mind came to a startling conclusion.

"I have a sweetheart, Mamó, and I am going to ask for her hand soon after she turns twenty-one. She is the most beautiful girl in

New York and has the kindest nature. I know you would approve of her," Tom reached inside his jacket. "See for yourself how pretty she is."

Mary squeezed Tom's hand, smiling as best she could at the photograph of the pretty young woman who had captured her grandson's heart. She nodded her approval but to the young man's surprise, rang the bell over her bed.

"What is it, Mamó? Are you thirsty?" Tom picked up the spouted bowl from the bedside table.

"What's all the bell-ringing about, love?" James inquired as he came through the door. "Has our Tom worn you out, already?"

Letting go of the string, Mary cupped her grandson's chin in her good hand and turned his face towards her husband. Tom did not resist, even though he had no idea what was troubling her, but he was beginning to regret having confided in her about his sweetheart.

Unlike his grandson, James sensed immediately what was bothering Mary and he held the door open wide.

"Yes, love. I can see what a fine man our Tom has turned out to be. Why don't you have a wee rest now and let him take a sup of tea? I'll stay here a while and keep you company."

James watched Mary's eyes follow their puzzled grandson to the door and as soon as they were alone, a low mumbling broke the silence. It wasn't too difficult for him to guess what name was being uttered and he patted his wife's hand and looked sadly into her anxious eyes.

"Yes, Mary. He is the very spit of young George. And how can that be, you may well ask? Indeed, I've pondered the same question myself and can come to only one conclusion. Mary-Anne no more adopted her son than we did her. Blood brothers could not look more alike than those two boys. I daresay there will be much talk over this among the neighbours," James sighed.

Sitting next to the bed, his head bowed and lost in thought, James was at first oblivious to the bell ringing overhead. He looked up just as Mary-Anne came running through the door.

"I think your ma has need of the bedpan. Is that not so, Mary?" James was gone before either woman could answer.

There was something strange about the way her mother looked at her but Mary-Anne put it down to tiredness due to the excitement of having visitors. By the time she came back into the parlour, James had left the house to spend the night fishing, taking Tom with him. Catherine was sitting by the stove, hands folded in her lap, as she watched her sleeping aunt.

"Maggie sleeps a lot, doesn't she?"

"Thank goodness for small mercies," replied Mary-Anne.

"You wouldn't put her in the workhouse, would you?" asked Catherine.

"Can you see Da letting me do that? Of course I wouldn't, she knows I'm only speaking in jest."

Catherine fidgeted in her chair, trying to find the right words to voice what she had been thinking all evening.

"We need to talk about something, Mary-Anne. Our sons bear an uncanny resemblance to each other, do you not think so?"

Mary-Anne stood over Maggie, listening to the rhythm of her breathing. When she was satisfied that her aunt was definitely asleep, she sat in the matching fireside chair opposite her sister.

"Are you going to tell me Patrick is not Tom's father?"

"Well, you don't have to be so blunt about it," Catherine snapped back. "That's not all I've been thinking about, Mary-Anne. There's no mistaking our sons share the same father and only you and I would come to that conclusion – for obvious reasons. Everyone else will think the resemblance between them must come from their mothers, that would be us, Mary-Anne. Do you understand what that means?"

"But I adopted George and I have the papers to prove it, Catherine. And I have his birth certificate with the name of his mother clearly stated on it. Just his mother, mind – no father. If I have to, I *will* reveal his name, although I swore an oath of secrecy about that."

Mary-Anne waited until her words sunk in before continuing.

"How shall you explain the fact that my adopted son and his cousin could not look more alike if they were brothers? Our sons must surely be thinking the same thing?"

"Ever since Tom passed the height of his father – I mean, Patrick – I have been telling people he takes after Ma's side of the family.

Remember how she used to say what a fine tall man her own father was. Sure, he died before any of us were born. Nobody here has ever seen him to say otherwise, except for Da and Aunt Maggie."

Catherine could see that her sister was thinking deeply about what she had said and assumed her next words would be an admittance that she was George's birth mother.

"Are you asking me to pretend that I gave birth to my adopted son when I know for certain it is *you* who has been living a lie all these years?"

Catherine felt trapped, like a prisoner in the dock, as her sister's words echoed accusingly in her head. She wrung her hands together and searched for the right thing to say that would reach Mary-Anne's conscience.

"But it's the truth, isn't it? I know how dangerous that man, that so-called doctor, can be. He attacked me in the home of my employer, in my own room, Mary-Anne. That is why I had to leave so suddenly. When that monster arrived here, in Blackrock, I feared he might try and take Tom away from me. It broke my heart to see you in his company but there was no way of warning you. I did try. Do you not remember?"

"You cannot even bring yourself to utter his name, can you? Gilmore. Say it, Catherine. Doctor Gilmore is the father of your first born child. I knew it the minute I saw our sons walk through that door together. And don't expect me to believe he attacked you. He could have any woman he desired, rich or poor, so why would he need to force himself upon *you*?"

A gasp from across the room reminded the women that they were not alone. Mary-Anne stood over their aunt for a few seconds, watching her closely, "She's still asleep, thank goodness."

"Then you admit it. He is your son's father, too," Catherine carried on the conversation in a low voice.

"I am not afraid to acknowledge the fact that Doctor Gilmore is the man who fathered George. But I will swear on my son's life that I am not the woman who gave birth to him," Mary-Anne's eyes were ablaze. "And I have a legal document to prove it."

Catherine saw in an instant the damage such a revelation would do to her family and her marriage. The pain would be unbearable for Patrick and she doubted he would ever forgive her, even if he could bring himself to understand her reasons for keeping such a dreadful secret from him.

"I can see you are still as hard-hearted as ever, Mary-Anne, so I will not waste any more of my breath in trying to reason with you."

Catherine spoke in a calm voice that belied the racing of her heart. She walked slowly to the door and opened it wide, resisting the urge to grab hold of her sister and push her through it.

"Sergeant Broderick must be wondering when you are returning home, the hour is quite late. I am well capable of taking care of Ma should she need anything."

Mary-Anne wrapped her cape around her shoulders and took her time in fixing her bonnet in place. Glancing across at her aunt before leaving the house, she regretted the fact that Maggie had been asleep and there was no one to verify what Catherine had just revealed. She looked into her sister's eyes one last time and saw a coldness that was totally out of character.

"Goodnight, Catherine."

Should the house have been empty, Catherine would have slammed the door shut, she was so full of rage and fear, her head throbbing with pain. So many regrets came to mind in the time it took for her to walk the few steps across the parlour to bank the fire for the night.

As her eyes swept over the familiar objects in the room, Catherine remembered the exact spot they had been standing on when she told her father she had been attacked by a stranger and found herself pregnant with Tom. She remembered her relief when he took her in his arms to comfort her and promised never to reveal such a dreadful secret to her husband. Although it terrified Catherine, knowing her son might now discover the circumstances of his birth, she could not bear to think about Patrick finding out such a thing.

Catherine blew a kiss towards her aunt before leaving the parlour, not wanting to touch her and risk disturbing her slumber. Her father had told her he would be sleeping upstairs with Tom while they were visiting and Catherine had been looking forward to lying beside her mother, reliving her childhood, when nightmares would send her running into her parents' bed.

As she slipped under the covers, the warmth of her mother's body reached her, taking the edge off her anxiety and soothing her throbbing head. She knew that sleep would not come easy but Catherine was happy at that moment to be in a safe place, away from everything that threatened to tear her world apart.

In the quietness of the parlour, Maggie opened her eyes and listened for a few seconds to the sound of the waves lapping on the shore.

"Well now, what do you make of that?" she asked the empty room.

CHAPTER TWELVE

Patrick removed his cap as he waited for his brother-in-law's door to open.

"Good evening Thomas. Is our Ellen about?"

"Come in, come in, Patrick. She's gone to bed. What has you out at this hour, do you not have work in the morning?"

"I'm sorry, were you about to retire?"

"Not just yet, Lily is making us a cup of tea. You look as if you need one yourself."

Patrick followed his brother-in-law into the kitchen and greeted Lily.

"You timed that well, Patrick. Shall we have it here at the table?" she asked, then noticed his agitation. "Or would you like to speak to Thomas in private? I can bring a tray into the parlour."

"Here is grand, thank you Lily. I have a question I must ask both of you," Patrick reached into his pocket. "But first, you must read this letter to us, Thomas."

The couple recognized the envelope addressed to their nephew.

"Did you not get Maisie to read it, Patrick? This has been opened."

"I did, Thomas. She is going to send a telegraph to Tom in the morning. Please read aloud what is in that letter."

Lily rose from the table, "I'm not sure I should be listening to your son's business, Patrick. I'll be off to my bed."

"Please stay, Lily. Tom would not be concerned about your presence and you might be able to shed some light on something that has been troubling me, ever since Maisie read out that letter."

As Thomas proceeded to read aloud the solicitor's words, Patrick watched their reactions closely. The look of surprise on his brother-in-law's face was completely different to the expression on Lily's. Although she kept her head down it was plain to see how nervous she was, repeatedly turning her cup around on its saucer.

As the letter came to an end, Thomas let out a low whistle and looked across the table at Patrick. He noticed him staring at Lily, who seemed to become even more anxious now that she had attracted the attention of both men.

"You knew, Lily. Do not deny it. When did Catherine share her little secret with you? You must think me such a fool. Then again, I'm sure you had friends in your past life who played the same trick on unsuspecting simpletons like myself. Before you met Thomas, of course."

Patrick was alluding to how Lily had been rescued by his brother-in-law from a life of prostitution. The people who had given her shelter when she was orphaned at a tender age had taken advantage of her.

"Listen here, Patrick, that's no way to speak to my wife. I think you owe her an apology."

"No, Thomas. Patrick has every right to feel hurt. I'm sorry, I was sworn to secrecy," said Lily.

A dreadful silence descended on them and it took all of Patrick's strength to break it.

"Do you know who Tom's father is, Lily?"

"You are, Patrick. You have been the best father a child could ask for. Do you think Tom will love you any less if he finds out that he came from another man's seed?"

"You haven't answered his question, Lily. Patrick deserves the truth," Thomas urged.

He had adopted his own son, Jeremiah, but loved him just as much as he did Eliza, his daughter by his first wife, who had died not long after the birth. If Lily had been able to bear a child, Jeremiah would still be as important to them and loved just as equally. It was different for Patrick, he had married Catherine not knowing she carried another man's child, and had reared Tom believing he was his own flesh and blood.

"I will never stop loving my son. You are right in what you say, Lily – Tom will always be *my* son. When he comes home we shall have to come to terms with this news together. It is not my feelings toward Tom that are causing me pain, it's his mother. How could she deceive me in such a callous way? And for so many years."

"Lily, did you know that this man . . ." Thomas glanced at the letter he was still holding, "This Doctor Gilmore fellow. Was he the man that assaulted Catherine?"

"Assaulted? Is that what she told you, Thomas? And you believed her?" asked Patrick.

"Catherine never confided in me. It was Lily who told me that she had been attacked by a stranger, but now I'm not sure what to think," admitted Thomas.

"Enough," Lily snapped. "Both of you need to listen to what I'm about to tell you and stop casting the blame on poor Catherine. It was on one of our visits to Ireland that she told me of her terrible secret, you might remember how distressed she was at the time, Patrick. Gilmore had brought his ailing wife to Blackrock to improve her health and Catherine was desperate to get away from him," Lily allowed this to sink in before continuing. "In fact, that was when she made up her mind to come to America. Do you recall the occasion? She was sitting on the wall crying, outside your house, and she told you it was Mary-Anne had upset her."

Patrick nodded but couldn't speak.

"I remember another time, when she took a turn in the street and we brought her to our hotel room," said Thomas. "Was that when she confided in you, Lily?"

"Yes, it was. Catherine told me how Gilmore had attacked her in the house in England where she was a lady's maid. He was a guest of the family at the time. That was why she gave up her work, Thomas, and moved in with your aunt Rose. Who would believe the word of a servant against a doctor?"

Lily could see that her words were being taken in by Patrick and carried on speaking. She explained how Rose had talked Catherine into marrying him when she found out about the pregnancy.

"After all, you were courting her at the time," said Lily, "And she had grown very fond of you."

"But why did you or Catherine not tell one of us – or better still, both of us – about Gilmore, when he was in Blackrock. We would have thrashed the scoundrel to within an inch of his life," shouted Thomas.

"Shhh. Keep your voice down. You'll waken the house," said Lily. "And that's exactly why we couldn't say a word to either of you. Do you think a man such as he would take a beating and then crawl away with his tail between his legs? Both of you would have ended up in jail, or worse, swinging for your trouble."

Lily paused for breath, hoping the men would understand the need for discretion at the time.

"We decided it would be for the best if the past stayed in the past and everyone got on with their lives," she said.

Patrick picked up the envelope from the table and snatched the letter out of Thomas's hand.

"Unfortunately, the past has a way of catching up with us and revealing its dirty little secrets," Patrick felt a stab of remorse at the look of shame on his sister-in-law's face. "I have no quarrel with you, Lily. It was Catherine's place to tell me the truth and not let me find out at this late stage. In fact, I am grateful for your honesty tonight."

As Patrick took his coat from the back of the chair Lily put a hand on his arm.

"Don't leave just yet. You are far too upset," she said.

Thomas fetched his hat and coat from a stand in the hallway and returned to the kitchen, announcing that both of them needed some fresh air and a stiff drink.

"Do not wait up for me, Lily. I predict we have a long night ahead of us. Is that not so, Patrick?"

CHAPTER THIRTEEN

Catherine and her son had been in Blackrock just two days when Tom received a telegram from his sister in New York, informing him that a letter from a legal firm had arrived addressed to him. He had replied that she should read it and let him know what it was about. When the second telegram arrived from Maisie, it contained a message that puzzled the young man.

"Why would a stranger leave me something in his will?" Tom asked his grandfather.

Catherine had just come through the door, having returned from a visit to an old school friend. She almost collided with Mary-Anne, who was in a hurry to leave.

"I must be away. I shall see you later, Catherine. I have some lodgers who will be looking for their midday meal soon."

There was an excited air about her sister but Catherine was well used to Mary-Anne's erratic moods and thought nothing of it.

"What stranger? What's all this about a will, Tom?" she asked.

"I've received another telegram from Maisie, about that letter addressed to me."

When Tom stood next to his mother and held out the telegram to her, Catherine automatically took it but her hand began to shake.

"What does it say, Tom?" she asked, passing the paper back to him.

"That someone I've never even heard mention of has left me something in his will," Tom took the telegram from his mother. "Someone by the name of Gilmore. Doctor Gilmore. Do you know of this person, Ma?"

Maggie sat at the table, closely studying her niece's face and wondered what her response would be. From the conversation she had recently overheard between the two sisters, there was no mistaking the fact that the same man had fathered both Tom and George. She had a good memory where people were concerned and could recall with ease the face of the doctor who had taken Mary-Anne back to England with him all those years before, as a companion for his sick wife. Maggie, herself, had stood at the quayside in Dundalk and watched them depart.

"Why, he was one of the doctors that attended your birth, Tom. In fact, I do believe you were the very first baby he brought into the world. How generous of him to remember you in his will," Catherine explained. "It was Doctor Gilmore who employed Mary-Anne as a companion to his sick wife. Did she not recognize the name? After all, she lived with them until her mistress's death, rest her poor soul," Catherine struggled to keep her voice even and calm.

"That's strange. She never said, Ma. Well, I must have made a remarkable impression on him. Maybe he left me his snuffbox or some such memento."

"Yes, yes of course, Tom. It shall be something like that, I'm sure," Catherine replied.

Ever since the conversation with Mary-Anne about the paternity of their sons, Catherine had become even more determined that Tom would never find out the truth. If it meant that Mary-Anne's reputation was sullied, so be it. Whether or not she had given birth to young George, Catherine was convinced her sister had shared a bed with Gilmore – and done so willingly. The gossip already beginning to sweep through the village was about Mary-Anne, not Catherine.

******

Sergeant Broderick had known for a long time that the birth of his stepson, George, was the result of Doctor Gilmore's frequent adulterous acts with one of his domestic servants. Mary-Anne had sworn him to secrecy when she revealed this fact to him, not long after they had married.

She had signed a confidentiality agreement, drawn up by Gilmore's solicitor, that she would never disclose the identity of the boy's father. Mary-Anne had been paid well for her silence and for her guardianship of the young child. Sergeant Broderick was a very discreet man and his wife knew she could now trust him with another secret, one that involved her sister Catherine.

The sergeant reacted just as Mary-Anne expected he would, with little or no show of surprise or judgement. He merely replied that unless Catherine owned up to her affair with the doctor, the unmistakeable likeness between the boys would be taken as proof that

George was Mary-Anne's own flesh and blood. Being in possession of a document stating the identity of the young man's birth mother would make no difference to the gossip that was likely to ensue.

Although she had been young enough to bear a child when they married, Mary-Anne had never conceived in the years they had been together. At first, the sergeant had looked forward to producing offspring of his own, even though he had grown to love his stepson dearly. As the years went by and no pregnancies occurred, he resigned himself to the fact that his wife must have been of an age when conception would be more difficult. The significant amount of years between them may have also been a contributing factor, the sergeant being not far off his father-in-law's age.

Sergeant Broderick was grateful that Mary-Anne never complained nor fretted about their lack of children. In spite of having a strong mutual respect and love for one another, their relationship had never been one of great passion, the likes of which he could see with his parents-in-law. Since Mary's affliction with that first stroke, James's deep love for her had become even more obvious.

"You are not going to dish up a plate of bread and cheese for our guests, Mary-Anne. Surely they will expect a more substantial meal than that?"

"They had such a large breakfast this morning they told me their stomachs would be full for the day. I'll be making them a good supper when they return this evening, Sergeant," replied Mary-Anne.

"I see. So I take it that pitiful offering is for ourselves, is it?"

"There's some bacon hanging in the larder. You are well able to slice yourself a cut of it if you are that hungry." Mary-Anne patted his rounded belly, "Now that you've retired from labouring you don't need the half of what you put into that mouth of yours."

The sergeant laughed as he went to fetch the meat and shouted back that he was still a growing lad. On his return he found a very subdued wife, nursing a cup of tea in her hands, not even a bite taken out of the slice of buttered bread on her plate.

"Are you not hungry, my dear?"

Mary-Anne slowly shook her head. She had been trying to imagine Gilmore attacking her sister and come to the conclusion that such a thing would never have taken place. The man was indeed a bully, but an irresistibly handsome one. She herself had once been a slave to his charms. Mary-Anne had eventually become weary of his attention and when Gilmore grew tired of her, she considered it no great loss to find herself replaced by an exceptionally pretty, much younger domestic servant. Having a young child and a sick mistress to care for took up all of her time and energy.

"Catherine claims she was attacked by Doctor Gilmore but I cannot believe such a thing. The truth of it is, she was very young and fell under his spell, and she wouldn't be the first woman to do so. When my dear sister found out that she was with child, marrying Patrick Gallagher was the only thing she could do to save her reputation."

"Of course you, yourself, did not fall under the good doctor's spell, did you, Mary-Anne?"

It was difficult to tell if Sergeant Broderick was upset or angry, or just inquisitive. He had the ability to control his facial expression, no matter what emotion he felt, and his wife had never learned to read him very well in that regard.

"Of course I didn't. I was too busy tending my mistress. His poor wife was such a frail little woman, I grew quite fond of her."

Sergeant Broderick's face softened, "I was a soldier for a long time, Mary-Anne. I hope you are not under the impression that you are the only woman I have been intimate with."

"I am not so naïve as to think that, but I do believe I am the only woman, besides your mother, that you have truly loved. One man in a lifetime is plenty for me, Sergeant, so I do hope you intend on living to a ripe old age, for there'll not be anyone filling your shoes. I can promise you that."

Mary-Anne's husband studied her as she spoke about his demise with the same amount of concern she would give to a conversation on the weather. In fact, the threat of rain would produce far more emotion from her, as the clothes-line in the garden was constantly filled with freshly laundered bedlinen for her guests.

"I care not what men may have been before me or, indeed, what suitors you might attract as a widow. It's me that has you now, Mary-Anne, and that is all that matters."

CHAPTER FOURTEEN

Patrick stepped down from the upturned wooden crate, finally making eye contact with Thomas and Lily.

"Well, what do ye think? Be honest with me, I do not want to make a fool of myself in front of strangers. It's difficult enough to do so with family."

Lily embraced him tightly and Patrick was surprised to see her eyes glistening.

"It was the best speech I ever listened to. You were born to do this, Patrick," she said.

"Did you get Maisie to write it down for you?" asked Thomas.

Patrick felt a wave of humiliation hit him and glared at his brother-in-law, "Do you think me incapable of composing it on my own?"

"Stop being so sensitive, that's not what I was implying," said Thomas. "This is only the first of many such speeches and you need to keep a written record of each one. The newspapers will soon be asking to print some of them, or at the very least, quote from them."

"I'm sorry. No, I didn't think it necessary. I'll ask Maisie to do so this evening. Well? Are there any changes I should make? You can be honest with me, I promise not to snap your head off," Patrick's face lit up with a genuine smile.

"It's perfect the way it is. I wouldn't change a thing, not a word," the commendation was unmistakeable in Thomas's voice. "But there's just one thing you need to do when speaking – look directly at the crowd. Sweep your eyes across them and every so often let them linger on someone, as if you are talking only to that person, but just for a few seconds. Not long enough to embarrass the listener, but in order to make a connection with them. Do this with different people throughout the crowd until your speech ends. They will be the first to applaud you and everyone else will follow."

"Everyone except the hecklers, that is, but they won't bother me. Thank you for your advice, Thomas. I shall try to remember that but it won't be easy. My nerves will get the better of me, I know it."

"Confidence will come with practise, Patrick, you'll see. You have an amazing memory for the spoken word, a sharpness that may not have developed had you learned to read," said Thomas.

"I'm still determined to gain that skill. Maisie and Ellen are good teachers, although I fear my attempts at writing stretches their patience to its limit."

Thomas patted his brother-in-law's back, "All in good time, Patrick. All in good time."

Time was not something that Patrick had in abundance and as soon as his visitors left the apartment, he stepped back onto his crate. His voice, full of passion, resounded around the empty room as he picked out pieces of furniture to rest his eyes on, putting Thomas's advice into practise. At the end of his speech, Patrick collapsed onto the nearest chair, his energy spent by his heightened emotional state.

So much had changed for him in the past week that if he stopped to think about it for too long his head would spin. The realization that his marriage had been based on a lie had been painful enough in itself, but to know that one of his children was the offspring of another man was devastating.

Patrick knew he would have to channel his rage into something or he would end up trying to drown it with alcohol. At the quarry, he threw himself into his work with such force that his colleagues began to wonder if he had lost his mind. They all knew to pace themselves or they would never last a week. It was only when one of them approached him with a request to slow down, as he was making the rest of them look lazy, that Patrick took stock of what he was doing to himself.

The speech had come to him one night as he lay in bed drifting in and out of a restless sleep. He wasn't sure whether or not he dreamed most of it but knew it was his own composition and not something he had heard in the past. Rising before his daughters next morning, Patrick paced around his bedroom repeating his speech over and over in a low voice, until it was set like stone in his head.

Young Tom was due home by the end of the week, Catherine having decided to stay on and help nurse her mother. Patrick was glad he had made the decision not to reveal to his son in the telegram that his inheritance was a substantial amount. Such a thing would raise awkward questions that were far better dealt with once Tom was back home in New York.

Every time Patrick's heart softened towards his wife because of the grief she must be experiencing with her mother so gravely ill, his own pain would quickly take hold and smother any trace of sympathy he felt towards her. Patrick had no idea what information awaited his son at the law firm in New York, where he was to present himself to claim his inheritance. Whatever news was to be revealed, he felt in his heart that Tom should know the truth. Patrick's dilemma was in deciding whether or not to share his mother's dark secret with him before she came home, or keep him waiting until her arrival. There was a distinct possibility Tom's visit to the lawyer's office would take that decision out of his father's hands.

CHAPTER FIFTEEN

The day was one of mixed emotions for Catherine. Her sister Breege's visit had been the highlight but her son's impending departure the following morning cast a dark shadow over the siblings' reunion. As they walked arm in arm along the sea wall in the village, each one struggled to maintain the cheerful exchange of news that should have flowed easily between them after such a long absence.

"I'm sorry, I'm not much company am I, Breege?"

"I understand, Catherine. My own visits home of late have not been very pleasant experiences. It pains me to watch Da grieve so. Can you see it in his eyes? I can. Ma seems to have accepted her fate, especially now she has received the Last Rites."

"He won't speak of how he feels, not even to me. It's as if he's afraid to say the words in case they come true. How on earth will he cope when she's gone, Breege? I fear for him, truly I do," Catherine dabbed tears from her cheeks.

"He will have his family around him, even when you go back to America and I'm not here. Mary-Anne has been surprisingly good with Da, he brings out the softness in her. Have you not noticed that, yourself?" asked Breege.

Catherine nodded, "I have, and I'm thankful for it, but it still worries me that he might give up on life once Ma is gone. Many a good man has turned to drink for less."

"He will still have Maggie to care for, that will keep him from losing himself in his grief. Her legs may not work so well these days but the rest of her is as strong as a horse. Our aunt has a few good years left in her, Catherine, and Da will not abandon her in her old age." Breege quickened her pace, "Now, let's have ourselves a nice pot of tea and some cake in Mrs. Flynn's new tearoom. With any luck, our Mary-Anne will spy us going in or coming out."

The women laughed at the thought of being spotted supporting the competition by their sister. The new tearoom in Blackrock had been a bone of contention with Mary-Anne since its recent opening, and she never stopped complaining about the business it stole from her own establishment.

Once inside, the sisters were surprised to meet Tom, who had just purchased some tarts.

"Will you not join us, son?"

"Sorry Ma, I must be off. I promised Aunt Maggie I would come straight back with these pastries for her," the young man looked around before lowering his voice. "I must say, I felt a bit of a traitor, with your sister's tearoom only a few doors down, but now that I see you both here I don't feel so guilty. You mustn't worry, though. Your secret is safe with me."

Tom laughed and bade farewell to his mother and aunt, leaving them to place their order.

Maggie had a pot of tea brewing and the table set for them by the time her grandnephew returned from his mission. She took two of the pastries and placed them on a plate in the centre of the table, leaving two more in the paper they had been wrapped in.

"Who are we keeping the other two for, Aunt Maggie?" asked Tom.

"Well, there's one for your grandfather, of course, and there's one for Mary-Anne."

"Surely she will be livid that you have bought someone else's pastries," said Tom. "Has she not been complaining all week about one of her neighbours having the cheek to open up in competition with her, even draping the windows of their tearoom with a similar fabric and painting their door the same colour."

"Yes, I doubt that there's a person in the parish has not been made aware of Mary-Anne's feelings about the new tearoom," Maggie replied. "However, it was she who asked me to send you to purchase a pastry. I merely increased the order. Fancied a morsel for myself, purely out of curiosity, of course."

"But why would she support Mrs. Flynn's business? It doesn't make any sense."

"In times of war, Tom, you must know your enemy well and his weapons even better. After all, Mary-Anne is married to a soldier, is she not?"

Maggie took a bite from her pastry as she waited for this information to sink in. She was surprised at how good it tasted and wondered who the cook was, for she knew Mrs. Flynn could not bake to save her life. It was the sergeant who made the cakes for Mary-Anne, being the son of a baker he had acquired that particular skill early in life.

"Oh my goodness, Tom, your aunt will not be happy about this. The pastry is melting in my mouth. I'm tempted to eat the other two, to spare her the pain of it."

The young man took a bite out of his own tart, not stopping until he had polished it off. He was stabbing the crumbs left on his plate with his finger when James walked through the door, his clothing covered in dust from the wall he had been repairing all morning.

"I hope you've left me some of whatever you're devouring with such gusto, Tom. I take it Annie has been to drop off some lunch for us."

Maggie looked up at the clock and frowned.

"She hasn't arrived yet, James. Go and clean yourself up before she gets here. Something must have delayed her."

Carrying a jug of water up to the room he had been sharing with his grandson, James replied that he would be relieved to wash the grime from his face and hands and might even change his shirt, as he was finished working for the day.

Tom watched his grandfather climb the stairs and a sharp stab of homesickness hit him.

"Ma always insists on Da changing out of his dusty clothes as soon as he comes home from the quarry. She won't let him near the table until he does so."

"And rightly so, Tom. You don't have to live in a grand house to have good manners," replied Maggie.

Annie arrived, carrying a wicker basket, just as James came down the stairs.

"Ah, you're a sight for sore eyes, love. I'm so hungry I could eat a horse," he said, rubbing his hands together.

"Before you eat a mouthful of Annie's food you must taste this pastry we've been saving for you, James," Maggie's eyes had a glint in them as she spoke.

James did as he was told. "Have you made this, yourself, Maggie? I think you might have some competition, Annie, love."

As she explained where the pastry had come from, Maggie noticed how quiet the younger woman had become and offered her a piece of the one she had saved for Mary-Anne.

Annie tasted a sample and became quite agitated. "Do you think it wise to give Mary-Anne that pastry? Surely she is upset enough as it is, with Mrs. Flynn's tearoom drawing away her custom."

"I have no choice but to keep it for her, Annie. For it was she who gave me the money to send young Tom to fetch it."

"Oh Maggie, I am in a heap of trouble now, that's my pastry, I know it is," Annie was distraught. "This is Jamie's doing, I'll wager. I have been making tarts from a large jar of rhubarb preserve that Jamie brought home last week. He said Mrs. Flynn gave it to him in exchange for some of his catch. I was thinking the tarts were disappearing too quickly, but sure, you know our Jamie and his appetite."

Maggie burst out laughing and couldn't stop. James fought hard to keep a straight face but when he saw Tom's head bent low and his shoulders begin to shake, it was all too much for him. The sound of the bell ringing from the bedroom caught James's attention and he left their company to see what Mary needed. No doubt she heard the laughter coming from the parlour and curiosity had overcome her.

"I'm surprised that Mary-Anne has not already guessed who Mrs. Flynn has cooking for her," said Maggie. "She'll be as cross as a swarm of angry bees when she finds out. Oh, Annie, your Jamie has been up to his old tricks again, finding ways to get under his sister's skin. No doubt about it, this is his best one yet."

"I wish I could see the funny side of it but I cannot," Annie scolded. "Just when things seem to be settling down between those two, one of them does something to upset the other and the bickering starts up again. If you'll excuse me I'll be off home to drag that husband of mine out of his bed and give him a piece of my mind."

"Be sure to get the price of your pastries out of him first, before you kill him," Maggie shouted after Annie as she bolted out of the house in a rage.

James laughed as hard as ever in telling his wife about the pastries and it did them both a world of good.

"It's been a long time since we had tears of laughter running down our cheeks, my love. Though I daresay our Jamie will have tears of a different nature when Annie gets a hold of him," he said.

Mary squeezed her husband's hand and drank in every inch of his face, happy to see the old familiar twinkle in the eyes she had been looking into for most of her life. The years seemed to melt away from him and she saw before her once more, the bashful teenage boy who stole a kiss from her at the bottom of a grassy hill in Monaghan.

It wasn't a fear of dying that kept Mary hanging on to life, for she had already prepared herself for that event. The doctor must have thought she was asleep when she overheard him tell James that he didn't know how she was still with them. At first, she was determined to see her daughter and grandson and knew her time would not come until their arrival from America. Even though she had been given the Last Rites, something was still keeping her from making that final journey.

As Mary listened to James's reminders of the many antics their youngest son had gotten up to over the years, she offered a silent prayer of thanks for having such a good husband by her side. They had been through plenty of hard times but always drew strength from one another. No doubt, there would be more trials ahead for James, and the thought of him facing them alone was distressing to Mary.

Although she only had movement in half of her face and just one of her eyes now remained fully open, James could see the worry in her expression and misread the reason for her fear.

"It is my opinion, Mary, no matter what the doctor may tell us, that you are on the mend, my love," he spoke soothingly. "There is no need to fear you may be taken in your sleep, for I know that's what has you awake throughout the night."

James was surprised to hear Mary utter some garbled words, she had not spoken much to him over the previous two days. He could make out she was telling him she was not afraid of death, but the rest of her words were incoherent and he put his ear closer to her mouth.

"Can you say that last bit again, love?"

Instead, Mary stroked his cheek with her good hand then ran her fingers through the curled hair at the nape of his neck. The old familiar gesture transported both of them back to the last time they had made love and James realized his wife's fear was not for herself but for him. He took hold of her hand and kissed it before placing it over his heart.

"You will always be with me, in here, Mary. I shall never feel alone as long as I carry our memories around with me."

Mary's face relaxed and James could see his words were having the desired effect. The thought entered his head that if ever there was a perfect moment for her to leave him, this was it. He gently turned her onto her side and climbed in under the covers behind her, drawing her body into the familiar curve of his own. Mary held onto his hand as he wound it around her waist and James buried his face in the bundle of soft hair, gathered into a loose bun by one of their daughters earlier that morning.

"Shall I tell you a story, my love? It might help you to sleep."

James felt his hand being squeezed and spoke of a sunny July morning in the neighbouring county of Monaghan, many years before, when two young teenagers went berry picking on Fraughan Sunday. He told of how a tumble down a grassy slope led to a cheeky kiss and the start of an adventure that sent them on a journey through life together. One that neither would have swapped for all the tea in China.

The creak of the door alerted James to someone's presence and he lifted his head to see who it was. Catherine stood silently in the doorway, not wanting to interrupt but worried that her father might be hungry.

"Is your Ma asleep?" James whispered.

Catherine nodded and stepped toward the bed to help him out of it. Her mother lay so still, it looked as if she might have passed away in her sleep. Without thinking, she placed the back of her hand under Mary's nose.

"She's only sleeping, love. We won't wake her just yet, the sleep will do her more good than food. But as for me, if I do not put something into my belly soon, I fear I might collapse with the hunger."

CHAPTER SIXTEEN

"That was a fine supper, Maisie. I barely notice your mother's absence, at least my stomach doesn't."

"Don't pretend you're not missing her, I know you better than that, Da. I'm sure she won't be far behind our Tom when he arrives next week," the young woman stood up to clear the table. "Well, I'll be off to bed as soon as I've washed these dishes. I have a book I'm trying to finish and having the bed to myself is a luxury I intend making the most of, with our Ellen spending another night at Thomas and Lily's – and none of Tom's snores coming from behind the curtain on the other side of the room."

"Are you sorry we never moved to a bigger place?" asked Patrick. "At least your brother would have his own room if we had done so."

"Not a bit, think of all the money you saved in rent. Sure, there's no need to be moving now, Da. It won't be long before there's just yourself and Ma here, what would you need three bedrooms for then?"

"We'll be taking in lodgers when that time comes, like everyone else does. Everyone except your uncle Thomas, that is. His work as an editor brings him a steady income and his reporting adds nicely to it. Besides, Ellen spends so much time at his place she may as well be lodging there."

"She says it's because she can study better having a room to herself but I know exactly why she likes to be there, and it has nothing to do with books," said Maisie.

Patrick held his breath, he wasn't ready to hear that his youngest was thinking of a suitor.

"It's their indoor privy has our Ellen visiting so often. With Thomas and Lily having one on each floor of their building there's less people sharing it. And they have a proper bath," Maisie stacked the clean plates on a shelf as she spoke.

With a sigh of relief, Patrick agreed with his daughter and said he couldn't blame Ellen for wanting such a luxury.

"Even so, Maisie, our building is a good clean one with no overcrowding and we should be grateful for that. The landlord has always been good to his tenants and Mrs. Jeffries keeps the place as clean as a whistle. You won't find a trail of ash and rubbish running through the hallways like I've seen in other buildings. It would take more than an indoor privy to entice me to move from here."

Patrick was referring to the middle-aged widow who lived rent free in a small room in exchange for caretaking duties.

"What you say is true, Da. We could be living in Mulberry Street. And if that were so, then Thomas and Lily would be seeing a lot more of me, too."

Maisie kissed her father goodnight and went into her room, eager to begin the next chapter in the book she was reading. It wasn't long before she was stretched out in her bed, totally absorbed in the fictitious world of a dime novel. The muffled voice coming from the far side of the apartment told the young woman that her father was giving another one of his speeches – to the four walls of his bedroom. It didn't distract from her reading but was more of a comforting sound, one she was fast becoming used to.

******

The policemen patrolling the park the following evening would never have described Patrick's speech as comforting. In fact, it incensed them to the point of chasing him through the city until they lost sight of him. Patrick was both angry and exhilarated. The adrenaline rush of the chase had made him feel youthful and full of spirit, but he was annoyed that his well-rehearsed speech had been cut short by the arrival of the law.

To remind himself of the conditions many of his countrymen had first lived in on their arrival in New York and to keep the fire of indignation burning in his chest, Patrick made his way to Mulberry Street and The Bend. The tenement slum in that particular area was due to be demolished and replaced with a public park.

A Chinese family were being evicted just as he arrived, their two young children screaming in fear at the sight of their father being pushed from one brutish thug to another. There were two other men standing around watching, one of them with a firm hold of the children's mother as she struggled to break free and go to her husband's aid. The young man was shouting something in Chinese but

96

his outbursts only drew more blows from his assailants.

Patrick could not turn a blind eye as he knew the rest of the street had done. Normally there would have been women sitting on doorsteps gossiping about the neighbours who had not joined them that evening. Children should have been chasing each other in and out of the grim tenements while their fathers made a swipe at each one as they screeched past them.

Instead, the streets were empty but the windows were full of eyes, watching from their darkened rooms. As soon as he grasped hold of the raised fist of one of the assailants Patrick felt something heavy strike the back of his head and sank to his knees. He curled up into a ball, trying to protect his body from the blows and kicks that followed and was relieved to hear a familiar voice shout out that it was one of their own they were beating to a pulp.

The pounding stopped and Patrick heard the sound of boots scattering in all directions as a pair of hands went under his armpits and dragged him to his feet. One of his brows had a deep gash and blood was beginning to congeal over his eye. Patrick was given a cloth by the young Chinese woman and when he thanked her, she gave a shy nod before running back to join her family, who stood nearby surrounded by their meagre possessions.

"You were lucky I came along when I did, Patrick. Those thugs weren't too pleased with you interfering in their business like that. You might have found yourself at the bottom of the Hudson for your trouble."

Patrick shook the hand of his rescuer, recognizing him as one of the men who worked the same quarry as himself.

"I'm much obliged to you, really I am. I just couldn't walk on as if nothing was happening, that's what's wrong with everyone. People are not prepared to stand up for each other against oppression and injustice."

The man looked across at the Chinese family, still huddled in the same spot as if waiting for instructions as to what they should do next.

"They're not like us," he said in a low voice. "They're not even Christian. They shouldn't be here at all."

"Do you think those brutes that evicted them acted like Christians?"

A shrug of the shoulders was enough of a response to tell Patrick it was useless to carry on the conversation. He patted his work colleague on the back and thanked him again for stepping in before any physical harm had been done to the frightened couple or their children.

"They wouldn't have done too much damage to them, they were just making sure they won't come back. You were in far more danger than they were, Patrick, and if I were you I would be on my way now, before they change their minds and come back to finish what they started."

"Will you be safe enough yourself, or do you think they will hold a grudge against you for interfering?" asked Patrick.

"I don't live here anymore, I was on my way to visit a friend but I think it might be wise for me to postpone that for a week or so. Take care, Patrick, and head for home now, while you still can."

As he watched the man walk briskly towards the end of the street Patrick felt four sets of eyes on him. Pressing the cloth firmly against his brow to stem a fresh flow of blood, he turned to face the Chinese family and gave them a nervous smile. Without uttering a word, Patrick gestured for them to follow him as he quickly walked back the way he had come, in the direction of home.

CHAPTER SEVENTEEN

It had not been as difficult to wave goodbye to her son at the quayside in Dundalk as Catherine had expected. Although she was sad to see him go, she knew it would be better for him to get home and back into his normal routine. She had been surprised by Tom's acceptance of her explanation as to why he might have been remembered in the will of a doctor who had delivered him. Catherine prayed that Patrick's curiosity would be as easily satisfied and hoped there would be no letter from Gilmore declaring the real reason behind his apparent generosity.

"You're very quiet, love. Missing Tom already, are you?" James's voice cut into his daughter's thoughts.

Catherine sighed, "I'm sure you know how it feels, Da, with the amount of goodbyes you've had to say yourself over the years. Was it more painful for you to be on the boat looking back or standing on the quayside?"

James thought about this for a moment as he sipped the tea Maggie had made for them on their return. His sister had seen the sadness on both their faces as soon as they walked through the door and left father and daughter alone while she went into the back bedroom to sit with Mary.

"I would say standing on the quayside is much more difficult. If it is me that's leaving I can choose to come back but when I wave somebody off I never know for sure if I'll set eyes on them again. It's different for you, love, you'll be joining young Tom and the rest of the family soon enough," James patted his daughter's hand. "There are more ways to leave than on a boat, Catherine."

Before either of them could say another word, Maggie came stumbling back into the parlour as fast as her aching legs would carry her.

"Catherine, run and fetch Doctor McBride, your ma has taken another bad turn," she cried.

James rushed past his sister and stood at the end of his bed for a few seconds, tempted to call out to Mary or touch her in the hope that she might fight for her life, as she had done with each of the previous strokes she suffered. He tried to convince himself that it would be selfish on his part to beg her to stay with him when this might be her time to go. Maggie took that decision away from him by pushing her way past and grabbing hold of Mary's hands.

"Stay with us, love. Stay with us," she pleaded. "The doctor is on his way."

Snapping out of his uncertainty, James took his sister by the shoulders to lead her out of the room.

"We must let her go if it's her time, Maggie. Please leave us alone until the doctor arrives. I need you to do this for me."

For once, Maggie did as she was asked without any questions or resistance, even closing the door behind her to give them more privacy. James lifted Mary out of their bed and sat in the rocking chair, cradling her on his lap. He wrapped her in the quilt she and their daughters had made many years before and rocked back and forth, humming the tune of a song that had a special meaning to both of them, all the while never taking his eyes from his wife's face.

One of Mary's eyelids flickered and when her good eye half opened James thought he could see the trace of a smile, a hint of recognition. He kissed her forehead, as he had done so many times throughout their life together, and reminded her of departed loved ones who would be waiting for her to join them. He spoke endearingly of their twin boys, born too early, of his own and Mary's parents and of their beloved Pat and Annie. Many more faces flashed before his eyes but he had run out of courage and his words dried up.

Just as he was about to beg her not to go, James felt the weight of Mary's slight frame press heavily upon him and he tightened his grip, clutching her firmly against his chest.

On the other side of the door, Maggie heard a wail that sounded like a wounded animal. As she lifted the latch the words of a familiar song reached her ears, and she knew Mary had left them. On impulse, she ran across the room to open the window, as was the custom when a death occurred. In the soft glow from the lantern, Maggie saw tears glistening on her brother's cheeks as he struggled to finish the verse. Her voice was barely above a whisper as she helped him with the last few words of the song.

'So fill to me the parting glass.
Goodnight and joy be with you all.'

CHAPTER EIGHTEEN

Maisie was glowing inside, having spent the evening at a restaurant with Sean. It wasn't too often they dined in such an establishment but he had been promoted to foreman by the construction company he worked for and wanted to celebrate his good fortune. With an early start next morning, Sean declined her offer of some tea and bid her goodnight at the door to her apartment.

When she went inside Maisie smiled at the sight of her father asleep in his chair by the stove, touched by the fact that he had waited up for her. She tiptoed past him and opened the door to her bedroom, delighted to see an empty bed, a sign that her sister would be spending another night at their uncle's apartment. The luxury of not just a bed but a room to herself was something Maisie didn't experience too often and she was determined to make the most of it.

As Patrick continued sleeping, his daughter cut some slices of bread and covered them with the fruit preserve her mother had made before leaving for Ireland. While the tea was brewing Maisie gently shook her father to wake him and was surprised at how deeply he slept, especially in such an uncomfortable position.

"Da, I've made a wee bit of supper for you, the tea is nearly ready."

Patrick sat upright and rubbed his palms over his eyes to wake himself up more fully.

There was something he needed to tell Maisie but he was having difficulty remembering what it was.

The loud wail of a hungry infant startled both of them and father and daughter stared at each other for a few seconds.

"What was that?" asked Maisie. "It came from your bedroom."

Before he could stop her, she opened the door and startled the young Chinese woman who was sitting up in Patrick's bed with a baby at her breast. Next to her lay a sleeping man with a small child curled into his arms. Maisie backed out of the room as Patrick brushed past her to close the door, apologizing to the young mother as he did so.

"Come and sit down, love. I'll explain everything to you over a cup of tea," he held out a chair for Maisie.

"Da, there's a Chinese family in your bed."

Patrick poured their tea, "I know. I put them there. I'll sleep in Tom's bed tonight."

Once she had been told of the events of the evening, Maisie agreed that her father had done the right thing in giving the young family shelter.

"You mustn't let any of the neighbours see them, Da, or we shall be evicted ourselves. They cannot stay for too long."

"I know, but they have very little English, they're not long off the boat, Maisie. I remember well what that feels like, and *I* had the advantage of being able to speak the language. I'll not put them out into the street."

With his daughter agreeing the family needed their help, and reassuring him he had done the right thing, Patrick felt better about the situation.

The sound of a crying baby would quickly be noticed by the neighbours and it would not be long before questions were asked. After Maisie had gone to bed, Patrick spent a good hour thinking about this, sitting in his chair and sipping his lukewarm tea. He knew it was risky to help illegal immigrants, particularly if they were Chinese. There were some who would be only too happy to report him to the authorities if they got wind of what he was doing.

Patrick realized he would have to find someone in Chinatown to help him out. Because of racial discrimination the Chinese tended to stick together and for the most part, Chinatown had become self-supporting with its own way of doing things. Businesses had grown, providing jobs, and there was a certain amount of financial aid and social protection offered to its residents.

Finally admitting to himself that it was not something he could tackle alone, Patrick stood and stretched his legs before making for his son's bed and a much needed sleep. By the time he was under the covers he had decided who it was he should confide in. Thomas would know what to do and may even have contacts in Chinatown because of his work as a journalist.

The following evening, when Patrick arrived home from work, an unusual but pleasant aroma greeted him when he stepped inside his empty parlour. No sound came from the bedroom and the thought struck him that his

105

guests might have found themselves a place to stay without his help.

As he was examining the pot of food, kept warm on the stove, the creak of a door opening told Patrick he was not alone and he turned to see the young Chinese man standing at the kitchen table.

"Have you and your family eaten?" asked Patrick.

The only response was a puzzled look on the other man's face so Patrick resorted to communicating through gestures and held out the pot of food. The young man shook his head and patted his belly, indicating they had already eaten. He then proceeded to show Patrick a wooden box with separate compartments in it containing strange-smelling powders and seeds, which the Irishman assumed were for flavouring the food.

While Patrick tucked into a bowl of meat and vegetables, his house guest opened the oven door and removed some small flat rounds of bread. It occurred to Patrick it was the man and not his wife that had prepared the food.

"Are you a cook, is that how you mean to earn a living?" he asked.

After another five minutes of gesturing and miming, Patrick found out he had guessed correctly and by the taste and smell of the food, the man appeared to be a very good cook. The two men continued to communicate through a crude form of sign language and for the most part it worked, but left both of them feeling frustrated and drained. It seemed the family had been smuggled into America and given a piece of paper with a name and address written on it. Eventually, by showing the note to various people, the young man found the person he was looking for, or so he thought.

He had been told this man would bring him to Chinatown and assumed that was where he had taken them. Once money changed hands the couple were told to bring their children and belongings to the attic room at the top of the three story building from which they were subsequently evicted. They never even got the chance to step foot inside the door to their room but were chased back down the stairs by three angry men. The man who had taken their money was long gone by the time they reached the street.

"Do you mean to tell me ye only arrived here yesterday?" asked Patrick.

The young man shrugged his shoulders and frowned, unsure of the question.

"Never mind. Look, you stay here. No going outside. Understand?"

After a lot of hand signals and use of body language, Patrick was sure he had made his point about being discreet and keeping quiet. He was going to call on Thomas to get some advice and hopefully enlist his help in finding a safe place for these new, and most likely illegal, immigrants.

By the time he reached his brother-in-law's apartment, the dishes from their evening meal had been washed and put away. Patrick's youngest daughter, Ellen, was busy cutting fabric on the kitchen table under Lily's watchful eye.

"You might as well move in altogether, you're here that often," Patrick teased.

The two women stopped what they were doing and held each other's gaze until Lily nodded her head. Ellen turned to her father and gave him a nervous smile.

"As a matter of fact, Da, I have been meaning to speak with you about that very thing."

"You mean you want to live with your aunt and uncle and leave your poor old father all alone," Patrick heaved a sigh.

"But you still have Maisie, and Tom will be home the day after tomorrow, and Ma will be . . ."

Patrick held up his hands, "Ellen, I'm only teasing you, love. But are you sure Thomas and Lily don't mind having a lodger," he turned to look at his sister-in-law.

"Ellen is like a daughter to us, to both of us. Thomas missed out on having Eliza in his life and now that she lives so far away and has a family of her own to care for, we hardly see her from one end of the year to the other." Lily put her arm around her niece's shoulders, "Besides, I would love to have some female company. You would be doing me a great favour by allowing your daughter to live with us."

"Well now, I wouldn't want to be the cause of making the two of ye miserable, so you have my blessing, and Maisie's, too. I'm sure your sister will be delighted to have the bed all to herself, Ellen."

With the breath almost squeezed out of him by his daughter's excited embrace, Patrick left the women to their sewing and went into the parlour to join his brother-in-law. He congratulated Thomas on having a new member added to his family and offered to pay towards her keep.

"There is no need for any payment, sure Ellen is always doing something to lighten the load for Lily," Thomas pointed to his son. "And our Jeremiah could not have a finer teacher. Is that not so, young man?"

The boy lifted his head from a book he was reading and smiled, "Do you want to speak in private with Father, Uncle Patrick?"

"Thank you, Jeremiah. I have a very serious matter to discuss with your father, I'm sure the women will be glad of your company in the kitchen."

"I think I'll retire for the night, I would like to finish this book before the week is out. Goodnight Uncle Patrick. I'll see you at breakfast, Father."

"He's a fine young man, Thomas. Good manners and well-spoken, like yourself."

"I cannot take all the credit for how my son has turned out. His school makes sure that he behaves like a gentleman and Lily keeps him on his toes when he's at home."

"But there is nothing can influence a boy more than the good example his father sets for him, is there?" Patrick replied.

Thomas leaned forward and looked his brother-in-law in the eye, "This matter you've come to discuss must be very serious indeed, if you feel the need to flatter me."

Patrick drew his armchair closer to Thomas and spoke in a low voice as he told him about the young Chinese family he had given shelter to.

"You must know somebody who can help them. I was hoping you might have a contact in Chinatown?"

"The Chinese immigrants draw a lot of bad feelings upon themselves, Patrick. They work under conditions that no other men would put up with and for a lot less money, and they do not integrate with the rest of us."

"Did the Irish not do the same when they came here in their droves in the famine years? Many of them were unable to speak English and were taken advantage of in much the same way as this young Chinese couple. Are we not morally bound to help them, Thomas?"

"Are you aware of The Chinese Exclusion Act, Patrick?"

"I've never heard of it."

"It's a law that forbids citizenship to the Chinese, even if they have permits to work here. It also prohibits the immigration of the wives and children of Chinese labourers. That is why we see so few of them here – and why the family you harbour in your home must leave immediately. You would be in serious trouble should someone report it."

"But that's outrageous, Thomas. How can such a law be enforced against one race and not another?"

"Speaking out against the working conditions of the quarrymen is one thing, but I hope you are not considering taking on immigration authorities, too. That would have much worse consequences for you, Patrick."

"I know – I know. All I'm asking is that you help me find a safe place for *this* family. The children are so young, Thomas. After that, they are on their own, there is no more we can do for them. Please, think about it and let me know as soon as possible what your answer is."

"Ah, Patrick, you have already stabbed at my conscience. I can let you know right now that I'm willing to offer my assistance. We must be very discreet, and on no account is that family to leave your flat – not even to use the privy."

"I have already made that clear to them. I'm the one who's been emptying their chamber-pots when they have filled them. You should see how embarrassed they are when I do so."

CHAPTER NINETEEN

"She had one of the finest wakes I've seen in a long time," said Maggie.

"She did indeed," replied Catherine. "Ma was well liked, wasn't she?"

Both women stood side by side peering through the lace curtained window at James, who was sitting on the wall across from the cottage.

"Do you think he can see us watching him, Maggie?"

"How could anyone see through the likes of these? Even the light struggles to get in. Are the women in America as taken with such fancy window dressings as they are here, Catherine?"

"Of course they are, sure isn't it a sign of prosperity? Who wouldn't want to make a good impression on the neighbours? I have them on my own windows, as does Thomas and Lily."

After another five minutes of small talk they saw James stand and wave towards them. Catherine laughed and pulled back the curtain to return the salute. Both women knew where he was going.

"I'm worried about your father. He's been drinking far too much since the funeral. Have you not noticed it yourself?" Maggie shared a concern that had been playing on her mind.

Catherine admitted she, too, was concerned but hadn't the heart to chastise him over it.

"I've decided to stay on for another few weeks, Maggie. I cannot leave Da knowing he's hurting so much. They've been managing fine at home without me up to now, a wee bit longer won't do them any harm."

Maggie nodded and opened her mouth to say something then seemed to change her mind. Catherine noticed and assumed it was her father's drinking that was still worrying her aunt. She put an arm around the older woman's shoulder and kissed her cheek.

"You are not to be upsetting yourself over Da and his drinking. He needs time, that's all. Time heals all things, isn't that what they say?"

"Does it, Catherine? Is that what time has done for you? Do you think it will do the same for Patrick when he learns how you deceived him?" The words were out before Maggie could stop herself.

Catherine moved away from her aunt, turning her back on her as she did so, and tried desperately to keep control of her emotions. Torn between fear and grief, an overwhelming urge to scream the pain out of her heart took hold of her and Catherine sank to her knees as a cry of despair filled the room.

When Mary-Anne rushed into the cottage she found Maggie on the floor with her arms around her sobbing niece and assumed that her aunt had fallen and injured herself.

"Here, let me help you up. Did you have a fall, Aunt Maggie? Catherine, would you stop with your wailing and give me a hand."

"Leave her be. It wasn't me that fell, it was your sister," Maggie struggled to her feet with Mary-Anne's assistance. "I know all about that Gilmore fellow and the trouble he's caused the both of ye."

"I knew it wouldn't be long before she went running to you looking for pity," Mary-Anne chided.

"She never said a word to me, I'm the one asked her about it. The two of ye need to have a good old heart to heart. I overheard what ye both said that night, when ye thought I was asleep."

Catherine, who had calmed down, began to weep softly and Mary-Anne knelt on the floor in front of her.

"What do you say, Catherine? Maggie's right, we need to clear the air between us and this is as good a time as any. Da needs us to be strong for him."

The older woman watched her nieces go into their parents' bedroom, where they could speak in private without fear of interruption. She resisted the urge to offer any advice or even a word of encouragement. Maggie was afraid the wrong words might spoil the chance of a truce between the sisters. Raising her eyes to the ceiling, she spoke in a low voice.

"They're in your hands now, Mary. Do your best, love."

Maggie jumped as a movement outside the open door caught her attention but it didn't take long for her to regain her composure. She shuffled across the parlour to have a look and catch whoever had been spying on her. Her nephew, Jamie, was sitting in the same spot on the wall that his father had recently vacated.

"I'm sorry Aunt Maggie, I didn't mean to interrupt your prayers. Are my sisters about?"

"They're having a wee chat in private. Not an argument, for a change. At least, I hope that's what they're doing. They could be killing each other by now, for all I know, Jamie."

The young man helped his aunt take a seat on the lowest part of the wall.

"Well if they are, they're being very quiet about it. What has them wanting to spend time in each other's company all of a sudden?" he asked.

"Your sisters are worried about your father, as I am myself. I feared this might happen once your Ma was gone. He cannot face the day without fortifying himself with drink. I see him try every morning but by the time he's picked at the breakfast I set before him, the longing is in him again."

"That's what I came to speak with you about. Annie says we should have a family meeting about it first and then I should be the one to take him aside for a man to man talk. I'm not sure a son lecturing his father on the evils of drink is the right thing to do, though."

Maggie knew what Jamie was asking, "You mean you'd rather it was me who did the chastising."

"Da would take it better coming from someone closer in age to himself. Parents are not inclined to listen to advice from their children – even if it *is* good advice. Who am I to preach temperance to him, anyway? Sure I'm as fond of a drink as the next man."

115

"The trouble is, your father's reason for drinking has changed. He's using it to dull his pain. His heart is broken and I'm not so sure I can help him mend it."

"But can you help him live with it, before he drinks himself into the grave?" Jamie pleaded.

Maggie patted her nephew's hand, "My brother is a stubborn man and the more he is pressured the less likely he will be to listen. He has done this before, when you were too young to pay any heed to it, but it wasn't long before he came to his senses. Let's give him a wee bit more time and see how he fares, shall we?"

CHAPTER TWENTY

Although the family in America had been expecting bad news from Ireland any day, Mary McGrother's death hit them hard. When Tom arrived in New York he immediately arranged for a Mass to be said for his grandmother and even his unbelieving uncle Thomas attended. The family had come together for the day and Eliza, although expecting her third child, made the long journey from Annapolis in Maryland to be with her father at such a sad time. She would be staying with Thomas and Lily for a couple of days, before heading back home to her husband and two young children.

"It was lovely to see all the family together, although it's a pity that Ma wasn't here for it," Maisie said. "I think I'll have an early night, Da. I shall be working late at the factory tomorrow, to make up some of the time I took off today."

"I'll bring you in a cup of tea when the kettle boils, love." Patrick smiled when Maisie kissed his cheek and thanked him.

Once the tea was brewed Patrick took a tray in to his daughter and Tom could hear them speaking quietly to each other. The young man knew it wasn't just the loss of his grandmother that had him in such a sombre mood, it was the visit he had paid earlier in the week to the New York law firm appointed by Doctor Gilmore's solicitor in England to act on their behalf.

As soon as Patrick returned to sit back down at the table his son went to the stove to fetch the teapot.

"You seem overly subdued, Tom. Would you prefer something a wee bit stronger?"

The young man nodded his head as he reached for two glass tumblers, and a bottle of Jameson his father kept on the top shelf of the kitchen dresser. The whiskey was only taken down for special occasions.

Patrick had been alluding to a trip to a bar when he spoke of 'something stronger' and his son would usually have understood this. If drinking twelve year old Irish whiskey at home was his intention then something very serious was on his mind – and Patrick had a fair idea of what that might be.

"I think you'll need this as much as I do when I tell you about my visit to the lawyer," Tom held a glass out to his father. "I wanted to tell you about it straight away but we haven't had much chance to be alone. Now is as good a time as any."

This was the moment Patrick had been dreading and he desperately wanted to delay it for as long as possible.

"Did I tell you my good news, son? I've been asked to give a speech next week, and indoors at that."

"You told us about it this morning, Da. I get the impression you are trying to change the subject."

"What subject?" Patrick looked genuinely puzzled.

"The inheritance, Da. The money left to me by a complete stranger – or was he?"

Unable to look his son in the eye, Patrick leaned forward on his chair and focused on the golden liquid in his tumbler. A few more glasses would make it easier to answer the question he knew his son was about to ask, so he swallowed what was left in one gulp.

"Fill it to the brim this time, son," Patrick held out the empty glass.

The young man did as his father asked and watched as the second drink disappeared as fast as the first one. When Patrick once again gestured for a refill, Tom shook his head, his patience wearing thin.

"Have I done something to offend you, Da?" he asked.

This time, his father looked directly at him and gave a sad smile.

"No Tom, you have never in your life given me cause to take offence. I've been proud to call you my son since the day you were born."

Patrick waved his empty glass and gathered his thoughts as he watched his son reluctantly fill it.

"What is it you want to ask me, Tom?"

"I don't understand why I would inherit such a large amount of money from a man I've never heard mention of before. Ma told me that mine was the first birth Doctor Gilmore attended and that I must have made an impression on him, seeing as he remembered me in his will."

"How much did he leave you, Tom? The letter said a substantial amount."

"It's as well you are sitting down, for the shock almost knocked me over in that lawyer's office. The poor man had to fetch me a glass of water. I am five hundred pounds wealthier today than I was last week."

"Five hundred pounds?" Patrick thought he heard wrong. "Did you say, *five hundred pounds?*"

Tom nodded, still finding it hard to believe, himself. Listening to his father say it back to him was making it even more incredulous.

"And there was me, thinking I was going to inherit a snuff box, or some such trinket, as a memento," Tom poured himself another half glass of whiskey.

Patrick finished his own drink before taking the bottle from his son's hand and putting the cork back into it.

"I think we've both had enough of the *uisce beatha*. There's no point in beating around the bush, Tom. By rights it's your Ma should be telling you this, but seeing as she is in no hurry to come home, I think it only fair that you be told the truth sooner, rather than later."

"Was that man my father?"

Patrick nodded and his mouth went dry. He licked his lips, wishing he had not put the whiskey back on its shelf.

"It seems he was, Tom. My suspicions were aroused when I heard of your inheritance and I confronted your uncle Thomas about it. But he was as confused as myself. It seems your mother confided in Lily, though, just before we came to America. It was she who gave me the answers to my questions. Was there no reason given for such a large inheritance in the will?"

Tom shook his head, "I did ask but the lawyer told me I knew as much as he did about it."

"What I am about to tell you is not an easy thing to hear, son. From what I understand, your Ma was attacked by Gilmore not long after we began courting. When her aunt Rose found out she was with child, carrying you, Tom, she talked her into marrying me. Aren't I an awful eejit of a man, not even once did I question the fact that you arrived too early, yet as big and healthy as any new-born could be."

Both men stared into the open door of the stove, the hot coals glowing back at them.

"What will you do with all that money, Tom?"

"I'm going to return it. How can I accept anything from a man who would do such a thing to my mother?"

Patrick's heart swelled with pride at his son's words but he knew it was not a decision to be made in haste.

"Wait until your Ma gets home, will you at least do that, son?"

Tom laid his hand on Patrick's shoulder and gave a reassuring squeeze. "I will always be *your* son, Da. Nothing has changed the way I feel about that."

Patrick nodded and tried to swallow the lump of emotion lodged in his throat. If Tom had produced the money from Gilmore at that moment, he would gladly have helped him throw it into the stove.

CHAPTER TWENTY-ONE

A loud cheer went up followed by a round of applause, as Patrick's speech reached its climax. Tom stood at the outer edge of the crowd, transfixed at the scene played out before him.

"What a speech, Maisie. If I hadn't seen and heard it myself I would never have believed Da to be capable of such a thing."

A woman's voice behind them interrupted Tom's praise, "Is he your father, then?"

Maisie proudly replied that he was.

"Easy for him to rant against children under the age of fourteen working long hours. I'm a widow with five young ones to feed and my eldest is working since she was ten years old. Without my children's wage coming in we'd be on the streets."

"How many of them work, ma'am?" asked Maisie.

"Her brother's been working these past two years since he turned ten himself."

"What about the truant officers? Do they turn a blind eye when inspecting your children's place of work?" Tom asked.

"There's never been an inspection, as far as I know. It's only a small workshop. I press the close by night and my two children work there by day – and if your father wishes to put an end to that, then I'll send my three youngest to live with him and *he* can clothe and feed them."

There was no point in trying to win the woman over to her father's way of thinking so Maisie decided to meet her on common ground.

"Our parents worked as children, ma'am," she pointed to Patrick, who was winding down his speech. "His mother died in a workhouse after the family were evicted from their home. Da always says he came to America for a better life for his children and he made sure we all got our schooling. Didn't he, Tom?"

Maisie waited for her brother to respond with a nod, before continuing, "Our father wants more support from government for families such as yours. Did you not hear what he said at the beginning of his speech?"

"I don't waste my time listening to do-gooders spoutin' off about how they can solve all our problems. I was passing by and couldn't help but overhear what I did. Strong pair of lungs he has, I'll give him that," the woman smiled for the first time.

"You should hear him during the night, coughing the dust from the quarry out of those lungs. They don't sound so good then," said Tom.

The smile left the woman's face as quickly as it appeared, "Well, standing here prattling on won't get my children fed, I'll be off about my business."

"It was nice meeting you," Maisie called after the woman as she briskly walked away.

Without turning around, she raised a hand in response before disappearing into the crowd, her empty basket swinging by her side.

They were still looking in the direction the woman had gone when strong hands came down onto their shoulders. Maisie and Tom turned around to see their father smiling at them.

"Well, Tom? Give me your honest opinion?"

"I hung on every word you said, Da, and not because I'm your son. The crowd loved it, too. I thought my eardrums would burst with their cheering and applause."

"Good, good. I think we should celebrate with a tasty Sunday dinner," said Patrick.

Maisie assured her father she had cooked a joint of bacon and the vegetables were already prepared.

"We'll keep that for tomorrow, love. I was thinking we might eat at a restaurant today. Nothing too fancy, mind."

"I hope you don't mean a two-cent restaurant in The Bend, Da," joked Tom.

"What? Bring your sister to a stale-beer dive? I am happy to say that I never had the misfortune to frequent such dens of iniquity. Mark my words, it won't be long before The Bend is replaced by a nice green park, flowers and all. And one that welcomes all class of people, rich or poor."

Many parks had been off limits to those less well-off until the photojournalist, Jacob Riis, campaigned to have them built right in the middle of the worst areas.

"Don't encourage him, Tom, or he'll be off on another one of his speeches," Maisie scolded.

Patrick laughed at his daughter's good-natured jibe.

"Well, if we do not get a move on there won't be a seat left for us anywhere," he said. "I was thinking we might have some Italian food today."

The men laughed and placed Maisie in between them where she had to link their arms and run to keep up with their long strides. By the time they reached the newly opened Italian restaurant that Patrick guided them to, there was hardly a seat left. The dining area was the former living room of the house with a kitchen at the back and the family's sleeping quarters above. Thomas and Lily had eaten there the day before and recommended it to Patrick.

The trio were given such a warm greeting they felt more like friends of the family than patrons. People were moved around so they could sit together at a small table near the window and nobody seemed to mind the disruption. The buzz of Italian voices interspersed with hearty laughter created a homely, relaxing atmosphere.

"If the food is as good as the welcome we are in for a treat," noted Tom.

Patrick leaned back in his chair and nodded in agreement at his son. His mouth was already watering with the aroma that filled the room but when he saw the food on the other diner's plates it was all he could do not to drool.

"Well, Maisie, what do you think? Are you missing your bacon and cabbage?" he teased his daughter.

Although relishing the prospect of an Italian meal, Maisie felt the need to defend her own traditional Irish cuisine. She put on an air of indifference and shrugged her shoulders.

"I'll let you know after I've had a taste. I've eaten in places like this with Sean and the food isn't always as good as it smells," she was interrupted by a large bowl being placed in front of her.

Tom put his head close to his sister's and said in a low voice, "Admit it, your mouth has been watering since you put your foot through the door."

Because his son had spoken so quietly, Patrick didn't catch what was said but smiled when he saw Maisie playfully punch her brother in the arm. His heart warmed at the air of contentment about his children, which reaffirmed his belief that moving to America had been the best thing for his family. There were those who came and fared badly but many more had managed to break free from the slums that had been their only means of shelter on arrival, just as Patrick and Catherine had done.

"Da, have you ever tasted food as good as this? It's delicious," Tom spoke with his mouth full. "And the sauce – mmmmm."

Patrick had been looking at the street-scene through the window and barely noticed his food being placed on the table. He turned to face his son and laughed at the ring of tomato sauce encircling his mouth.

"Your dark hair might give you the look of an Italian, son, but your moustache betrays your Irish blood. Red as a tomato, it is."

Maisie instinctively wiped her mouth, too, "Bacon and cabbage might not be as flavoursome but it doesn't make half as much of a mess, does it?" she chided.

With full stomachs and the flavour of their food still lingering on their tongues, the three Gallaghers left the premises, having bade farewell to the middle-aged Italian woman who had cooked their meal. Both herself and her husband walked them to the door and stood waving after them.

"I didn't understand a word they said, did either of you?" asked Patrick.

Maisie shook her head, smiling.

"I got the impression they were happy to have our custom, though," Tom looked behind as he spoke. "They are still watching us – and waving," he returned the salute.

"Us immigrants are all the same, no matter what country we come from," said Patrick. "We need to support each other and that Italian couple are well aware of it. I fully intend on paying them another visit and not only because the food was so good. Although, I have to admit, I would be back tomorrow if Maisie had not gone to so much trouble with the bacon and cabbage."

After another round of teasing, Maisie announced that she would be spending the rest of the day with Sean and some friends, and invited her father and brother along. The men declined but said they would walk her to the arranged meeting place.

Having left his sister with her companions, Tom asked his father if he would like to go somewhere quiet for a drink, he had something he needed to discuss with him. As the two men took a short cut through a quiet alley they were grabbed from behind and dusty cloth bags forced over their heads.

Father and son were pushed and pulled between their assailants until a punch to the stomach forced Patrick's meal to come up and seep into the fabric covering his mouth. As quickly as it had begun, the attack ended, with the sound of heavy boots scurrying into the distance.

Tom pulled the bag from his head as he staggered to his feet and saw his father lying on the ground, coughing and struggling to raise himself.

"They're gone, Da," the young man knelt down on one knee. "Here, let me help you sit up. There were four of them but I didn't get a look at their faces. Do you know who they were? Or why they attacked us?"

Patrick picked up an empty flour bag from where it lay on the ground beside him. A red stain stood out against the white cotton cloth and when Tom saw it he grew even more concerned, asking his father if it was blood.

This made Patrick laugh, which set off another bout of coughing and spluttering and it took a minute for him to catch his breath.

"I'm alright, stop your fussing. That's not blood, but I have a feeling it's what frightened those cowards off – blast them for making me lose my dinner."

"You spewed up your meal?"

"I did, Tom, but it was the dust from the bag that set me coughing my guts up," Patrick did not want his son to know about the blow to his stomach.

"It's flour that was in those bags," Tom shook the white dust out of his hair. I daresay you inhaled a lungful of it and with you already suffering from your chest, I'm not surprised at your bout of coughing. Do you think you can get to your feet now? I'm worried those thugs might return."

Patrick leaned on his son to raise himself and saw their caps lying on the ground behind them. Gesturing for Tom to pick them up, he looked in the direction their assailants had fled.

"They won't be back. This has happened before, they're harmless enough and have more than likely been paid to scare me off. I reckon they got a fright when they saw that red stain and thought I was coughing up blood," Patrick laughed and coughed again. "They were sent to rough me up, not kill me."

"Sent by who? What do you mean it's happened before?"

Leaning once more on Tom's shoulder, Patrick assured him he was in no danger and suggested they carry on and have that drink.

"But first, let's brush this pesky dust from our clothes, son."

CHAPTER TWENTY-TWO

With the weather unusually warm and not a cloud in the sky, most of the younger children in the village were outdoors, playing in the street and on the sand, under the watchful eyes of their older sisters. The girls sat along the wall that separated the beach from the road, taking turns in reprimanding any of their young charges daring enough to get up to mischief. Annie and Jamie's children were among them, monitored by a neighbour's ten year-old daughter.

"Have you still not forgiven me for selling your pastries to Mrs. Flynn?" asked Jamie.

"It was wrong of you to do such a thing to your sister," Annie was busy preparing a midday meal with the fish her husband had caught the night before. "And to your wife."

Unable to see the set look on her face, Jamie took note of the stiffness in Annie's back and stood up from his chair to stretch his legs. A warm breeze carried the sounds of the street in through the open door of their cottage, tempting him to escape what appeared to be another lecture on family and loyalty.

Jamie was just about to make an excuse about mending a boat when his wife swung round to face him.

"I've been thinking on what you said, about not putting all my eggs in one basket," Annie sounded uneasy. "You might be right about that, so if you want to carry on supplying Mrs.

Flynn with whatever I manage to bake, then I won't stand in your way."

"I'm sorry, love, I couldn't hear what you were saying with all that noise coming in from the street. Could you repeat it for me?" Jamie struggled to keep a straight face.

"You heard me well and good, and if you didn't, then I might just change my mind. I could do without Mary-Anne's wrath coming down on my head."

Jamie was standing next to his wife in two seconds, assuring her that his sister would get used to the idea.

"You leave Mary-Anne to me, love. We've been keeping an easy enough truce since Ma's passing and I don't think a few pastries to Mrs. Flynn is going to change that. I'll tell her we need the money for the baby," Jamie patted the bump nestled between them.

"Have you had a word with your da, yet, about his drinking? It's at a bad enough stage when you have to be sent for to bring him home, Jamie. I've never known him to be that bad before."

"No, Annie, I haven't been able to bring myself to do it. I will, though, soon enough. Catherine asked me to have a 'man to man' with him. She says she can't go back to America while he's in such a bad way."

"Now is as good a time as ever," suggested Annie. "Why not bring him up to your ma's grave while he's still fairly sober? He's only ever gone up there maudlin with the drink. It might be the best place to make him come to his senses."

Jamie remembered how his mother always went to sit by Pat and Annie's grave whenever she was worried or saddened by something. On her return home, she would smile brightly, her mood obviously lighter.

"You might be right about that, love," Jamie kissed his wife, then bent low to whisper to their unborn child. "I'm off to get your grandfather in a fit state to meet you, little one. Wish me luck, I'll need it."

There were two places where James McGrother was likely to be found of late. A small guest house in the main street that was also a licensed premises, or Paddy Mac's. Jamie tried the guest house first, as it was nearer to him, and was told his father had been in earlier and left sober. The next stop was Paddy Mac's and if James wasn't there, then he could be anywhere.

Just a few days before, having been alerted by a neighbour, Catherine found her father hiding behind a hedge drinking whatever bit of alcohol he had managed to get his hands on. She helped him walk home, staggering under the weight, his clothes covered in vomit and reeking of cow dung. While he was sleeping it off, the family gathered to discuss what should be done, with Maggie being elected to try and talk sense into her younger brother. Although James had hung his head in shame, promising to ease off on the alcohol, he was as bad as ever the following evening and unable to take his place on his son's boat for a night of fishing.

It was a relief for Jamie to find his father in Paddy Mac's, where many of the older men in the village had gathered to get out of the sun's unseasonal heat, or so they claimed. James sat alone by the open fireplace staring at a neatly assembled structure of turf, kindling and twisted newspaper, ready to be ignited should the day turn cold. An invisible wall of seclusion surrounded him, a silent declaration of withdrawal.

Taking a deep breath, Jamie stepped through the open door and nodded to Johnny, Paddy Mac's son, who stood behind the bar with a sympathetic look on his face. Acknowledging the salutes of the other men present, the young fisherman took a chair from under one of the empty tables and dragged it after him, hoping the noise of wood scraping on flagstone would get his father's attention before he reached him.

James never even blinked. It wasn't that his mind was already dulled with alcohol but he was so deep in thought, the noise grating on the nerves of the other men present had no effect on him whatsoever.

Standing in front of his father, Jamie was aware of eyes stealing glances in his direction while the sound of whistling came from the stockroom behind the bar. Gradually, a murmur of renewed conversation began to filter through the silence and the atmosphere in Paddy Mac's returned to normal.

Jamie stood for a moment in front of his father, noting the empty glass cupped between his hands, the unlit fire still holding his gaze.

"Da, do you mind if I join you?"

When James shrugged his shoulders and held out his glass, Jamie called out to the barman, signalling for two drinks when he appeared behind the counter. He could tell by his quiet disposition that his father hadn't yet consumed a large amount of alcohol, for James had learned to pace himself through the day. A lack of money forced him to drink just enough porter to dull his pain and keep it that way until the night was upon him and he had an excuse to have something stronger, to help him sleep.

"Why do you do this to yourself, Da? And look what you're doing to Aunt Maggie, she's beside herself with worry over you – we all are."

James didn't reply but raised his head to nod at Johnny when two tankards were placed on a table nearby.

"I want you to come for a walk with me after we finish our drinks. Will you do that? It will do us both good to stretch our legs on the fine day that's in it," Jamie took a long, slow drink while awaiting a response.

"Where is it you want to take me, son?"

Anticipating a refusal, the question was so unexpected, it threw Jamie for a moment. He wasn't sure if he should mention the cemetery there and then or wait until they had set out on the road.

"I was thinking of doing a bit of weeding up at the graveyard. I'd be glad of the company, if you'd care to join me," Jamie held his breath.

James finished what was left in his glass in one long swallow and for the first time since his son had entered the premises, he looked directly at him.

"I suppose you want to have a word with your old man about his drinking."

Jamie began to protest but his father held up a hand.

"No need to get all flustered. I know Maggie has put you up to this and I understand her concern. Yours, too, son. So I'll go for that walk with you, up to your ma's grave, but you must leave me at the gate and come no further, hear?"

Jamie nodded his head and quickly paid for their drinks, eager to be off before his father had a chance to change his mind. This was the moment the whole family had been waiting for and he was sure it would be a turning point for the grieving man.

Once or twice on the journey to the cemetery, James brought a halt to their walk and seemed to be dealing with an inner conflict. He would take off his cap and scratch his head, frowning at the ground, then his face would suddenly relax and he would pick up the pace again. After James had done this a third time, his son was afraid he was changing his mind about visiting Mary's grave.

"Ma is going to like these, isn't she?" Jamie held out the posy of wild flowers he had been picking from the hedgerows along the way. "I remember she used to make us eat the leaves of this one at the first sign of a sniffle."

His father turned to look at the tiny yellow flower held out to him and smiled.

"What did she call it, Da?"

"That's scurvywort, son. Aunt Annie taught your ma everything she knew about wild plants and what they had the cure for. If she

135

were alive today I daresay good old Annie would know what plant I'm in need of myself."

Jamie wondered if his father was referring to his drinking or his grief but didn't want to cause any embarrassment by asking. Instead he chose another tiny blue flower, the name of which escaped them both. Their journey continued with the two men trying to recall the names of each flower in the slowly wilting posy, until the wall of the cemetery came into view.

To Jamie it was a welcome sight, relieved as he was to have gotten that far, but to his father it was a painful reminder of his grief. This was the first time since the funeral that James had been to Mary's grave in a sober condition. Before Jamie had joined him in Paddy Mac's, he had been nursing the same drink for over an hour and was now wishing he had a few more inside him. James asked his son to wait outside the wall and taking the posy from him, walked resolutely through the gate.

While his father was out of sight behind the ruin of the old church, Jamie stood on guard, determined not to let anyone get past him. He would delay them by keeping a conversation going, whether it be about the cost of flour or the latest gossip circulating the parish. The latter subject brought a smile to Jamie's face as he contemplated what that gossip might be and decided it must surely be about his sister Mary-Anne.

There was no mistaking the similarity between his two nephews, yet George had been adopted. Jamie was convinced that his sister was really the young man's mother and wondered what Sergeant Broderick must be thinking about it all. If Mary-Anne had indeed admitted it to her husband, surely there would have been some coolness between them, but they appeared to be as content as ever and not a bit bothered by what was being whispered behind their backs.

A shadow falling across his feet gave Jamie a start and he almost fell over when he heard the voice that greeted him.

"What make of a soldier are you, Jamie lad, letting me sneak up on you like that?" admonished Sergeant Broderick.

"Da is inside, he wanted to be alone. Have you been following us?"

"No, Jamie. In fact I've been trying to keep a good distance between us, ever since I turned a bend in the road and saw you both in front of me. I'm just out for a stroll in the fine weather."

"I get the impression there's more to your walk than you're saying but I wish you luck with whatever it is, Sergeant. We've not had much *activity* lately have we?"

The older man knew that Jamie was referring to Fenian assignments.

"Some of us are more active than others, lad. The fewer the better right now, but the day will come, mark my words. All that training won't be going to waste, if that's what you're thinking?"

Jamie didn't answer but suggested the sergeant continue his journey, in case his father should see them.

"I wouldn't want him to think we were talking about him," he said.

Sergeant Broderick agreed and tipped his cap to the younger man before setting off up the road with great purposeful strides.

But James had seen the two men and it forced him back to his wife's grave to avoid any discomfort for either them, or himself. He knew there must have been a family discussion about him and was not surprised when Jamie had suggested they take a walk.

"Well, Mary, I've come back again for a wee while. I don't suppose you want to hear another decade of the Rosary, do you, my love? No, I didn't think so."

James sat on the ground outside the neat row of whitewashed rocks surrounding the resting place of his beloved wife. He had wanted to recreate the small garden in front of their cottage that she had been so proud of. Glancing around, he was grateful to be alone and hoped his son would not get impatient and decide to join him.

"It's so peaceful here, Mary," James leaned against the headstone, giving in to the serenity.

The plot the family purchased was situated between two large yew trees, not far from the ruins of the old church and James knew Mary would have approved of it. He placed a hand on the headstone, covering the empty space below her name, and smiled sadly, knowing his own would fill it in time.

"I'm tired, my love. I haven't had a decent sleep since you left me and I'm truly sorry if I'm disappointing you in having to drink myself into a slumber every night. What must you be thinking of me, Mary? Our children are worried, I know that, but they don't need me anymore. I'm just a useless old man without you."

James bowed his head and saw dark patches form on the whitewashed stone in front of him. He allowed the scalding tears flow freely, unable to keep them in check any longer. That had only been possible with the help of alcohol but now it was time for the wall of grief to dissolve – and he shed a bucketful.

Aware that he was in a public place, James scanned his surroundings, listening for voices, but he was alone and thankful for it. Leaning on the headstone for support, he struggled to his feet, knees stiff and aching.

"It was a good time to pay you a visit, Mary, there's nobody about. Sure they're all having their midday meal, I daresay."

James took his folded cap from a pocket and placed it back onto his head, pulling the peak down low to conceal his red-rimmed eyes.

"Well, Mary, our Jamie will be starving by now. You know how he loves his food, so I'd best not keep him waiting any longer," James tenderly patted the headstone before turning towards the graveyard entrance.

Neither man was in the humour for conversation as they set out on the journey home but James felt the need to say something to put his son's mind at rest.

"That visit to your ma did me a power of good. I feel the better for it."

"And did you get rid of the weeds while you were there?" asked Jamie, a glint in his eye.

"I couldn't even find one. Why do you think that was, son?"

Jamie laughed and matched his father's steady pace, "Because Annie and Mary-Anne were up here yesterday and plucked up every last one of them."

Not caring how red his eyes were, James took the cap from his head and swatted his son with it, "You're not too big to get a thrashing from your old da. Keep that in mind for the next time you're tempted to dupe me."

CHAPTER TWENTY-THREE

Having read out the main stories to his father, Tom neatly folded the newspaper and placed it on a shelf, alongside a library book. When he saw that it was written for eight to ten-year-olds, he knew who had borrowed it.

"Ellen says your reading is coming along in leaps and bounds, Da. You'll be writing out your speeches before long, instead of dictating them. I don't know why you had me read you the newspaper, I could have helped you with the more difficult words."

"My eyes are always too tired for reading at this time of the evening, son," Patrick replied, then changed the subject. "I see there's been no sign of that Cavan man who jumped from the Brooklyn Bridge the other day. No mention of it in the papers anyway."

"What a foolhardy thing to do. The men he asked to watch him as he jumped should have grabbed hold of him and locked him up until he came to his senses."

"Well, Tom, not everyone is as sensible as you are. If there's one thing I can say in all honesty, it's that you never gave me a minute's worry in that regard."

"Speaking of worry, Da, I hope you're not going to be climbing up those skyscrapers now that Sean has you on his crew."

Tom was referring to the position that Maisie's young man had secured for Patrick when the quarry laid off a handful of men. On giving them their notice, the boss attributed the lay-offs to lack of funds, due to the financial depression the city had been in since 1893. But Patrick knew it was the company's way of getting rid of anyone too radical, and suspected his speeches on social change had come to their attention.

"Sean promised me there's enough work on the ground to keep me busy. It means less of a wage but I'd rather have a lighter pocket and live to spend it, Tom. I don't know how those men work at such heights, sometimes all they have to walk on is a plank of wood."

"Just looking at them up there is enough to make me dizzy, I don't know how Sean does it," added Tom.

"They're like monkeys, no doubt about it. I'm thankful I don't have to climb up there with them. I just have to make sure nobody lands on me," Patrick laughed. "Anyway, we'll manage a lot better when your ma gets back. She has a pile of mending waiting for her, poor Lily hasn't been able to keep up with it."

Catherine's sister-in-law had been helping her out with the small dressmaking business she ran from home. Since the financial crisis two years previously, many women were no longer ordering new outfits but having their old ones repaired instead. They even dropped in their men's clothes, and at times, Catherine found herself adjusting children's clothing she had originally made for an older child that was now being passed down to the next one.

This brought a fair amount of business to Catherine's door, and in her absence Lily had enlisted Ellen's help. Maisie's working week took up most of her time but her sister had shorter hours as a childminder, while she studied for her teaching certificates.

"Seems like the whole country has been either on strike or out of work this past twelve months, Da," Tom shifted nervously on his chair. "I could give you something to tide you over."

"I told you, son. I'll not touch a cent of that money, not even if my life depended on it," Patrick said firmly.

"Then why did you make me hold onto it? I was prepared to give it to a charity."

"We have already had this discussion, Tom. Wait until your ma gets back, we'll talk about it then."

With the tone of his father's voice signalling an end to the conversation, the young man brought up a topic he had been meaning to discuss since his return from Ireland.

"There's something else I need to tell you. I've already spoken of it to Ma, on our trip to Ireland. She told me I was to discuss it with you as soon as I got back to New York. I'm sorry I've left it this long but there never seemed to be a good time for it," Tom hesitated.

"Go on, son. Spit it out, whatever it is," Patrick was checking the laundry hanging over the stove.

"Will you sit down then, while I talk to you? You're like an old washer-woman," japed Tom.

Patrick took a seat at the table opposite his son, a mock frown on his face, "If I was waiting for any of my children to wash my clothes I'd be going to work looking like a tramp."

"You come home looking like one, what's the difference?" asked Tom, ducking to avoid a swipe from his father.

The two men carried on mocking each other until Patrick finally held up his hands in defeat.

"Enough," he said. "You've nagged me more in five minutes than your ma ever did in a year."

"Are you ready to hear what I have to say now?" asked Tom.

"I was ready five minutes ago," replied Patrick.

"If I *do* keep that money, I was thinking of putting some of it into Mr. McIntyre's business. He lost a lot of his savings when his bank failed and I know he's struggling to pay our wages. What do you think about that, Da?"

"It's Thomas you should be asking not me. What do I know about printing and newspapers? I have the reading ability of an eight-year-old. Does your uncle know how much you've inherited?"

Tom shook his head and told his father he hadn't revealed that to anyone but him. The young man looked perplexed as he nervously ran the end of a white tablecloth through his fingers. Made of Irish linen and decorated with embroidered shamrocks, it was one of two his mother brought back from a previous trip to Ireland, the other kept strictly for special occasions.

"Look," he stuck his thumb through a hole, "More mending for Ma."

"Son, is there something else on your mind? You've a desperate guilty look on your face."

"That's not guilt it's embarrassment," Tom squirmed. "It was easier to speak of it to Ma than to you. Well, I'll come straight out with it – I love Lottie McIntyre and she loves me. But her father doesn't know that, yet."

Patrick let out a low whistle, "The boss's daughter. You certainly know how to aim high, son, I'll give you that. Are you sure she loves you back? Has she said as much? You're not very experienced with women, Tom. Maybe you've misread a kind word or a friendly smile."

Tom shook his head, "No, I haven't misread anything. We've been passing notes to each other for two years now. Lottie started it off as a dare by one of her sisters and it followed on from that. We agreed to wait until she was twenty-one before I ask for her father's permission to call on her, and she's almost that now."

"I think you need to talk this over with your uncle Thomas. He knows your employer much better than either of us do. I know for a fact that McIntyre holds you in high regard, son, but as a good worker. He told me so himself on more than one occasion. I imagine investing your money in his business will greatly raise his opinion of you and entitle you to a fair share of it. You will have to make sure you get proper legal advice before you go signing over any money. Do you hear me, son?"

Nodding his head, Tom exhaled a long slow sigh of relief and noted the concern on his father's face. Now that he had revealed the reason for his interest in the business it was easier for him to speak freely of his plans.

"I know that Mr. McIntyre had been planning on spending more time with his wife, now that their daughters are grown, but the crisis of '83 has put paid to that. If he accepts my offer . . ."

"For his daughter or his business?" Patrick cut in.

Tom scowled, "For both, of course. Anyway, as I was saying, if he accepts my offer I think he should buy new machinery so that we can print colour images. People love colour, Da, it's the future of printing."

Patrick looked at his son's ink-stained hands, "How many years have you been working for him – ten, eleven?"

"Nearer to eleven."

"Your uncle Thomas started off like you when he lived in England, apprenticed to a printer. Look at him now, I daresay he'd find it mighty hard to recall the last time his hands were covered in ink. I always hoped you'd follow in his footsteps but you love those machines, don't you, son?"

"Me? A reporter? There'd be more chance of Maisie doing that," Tom examined his hands, then held them up. "There's no shame in a man earning a wage with these, is there? And no reason why it cannot be a decent wage, at that," Tom replied.

His father laughed, "Now you sound like me. No, son, a man's hands are just as important as his head. In fact, before there was ever a machine invented, a craftsman was a very important member of the community. Look what happened to the weavers – the machines took over and now they're called factory workers. They are still skilled men but today it's their employers that are looked upon as more valued members of the community."

"If I put money into Mr. McIntyre's business then everyone will benefit and we shall all keep our jobs," Tom gave his father a roguish smile, "And I might even become a *'valued member'* of the boss's family."

CHAPTER TWENTY-FOUR

Sergeant Broderick watched from the open back door as George went about his weekly chore of cleaning out the henhouse. The young man was as tall as himself and seemed to be still growing. Someone nudged him in the back and he looked around to find Mary-Anne standing behind, a wooden tray in her hands.

"The guests are gone off for the day so we have the place to ourselves, Sergeant," she nodded towards her son. "Now would be a good time for you to have that talk, don't you think?" she remarked.

They both stood watching him until he turned around and waved at them from the end of the garden. The sergeant almost regretted his promise to Mary-Anne that he would answer George's questions concerning the circumstances around his birth. It was a delicate matter for a woman to discuss with her son and although his wife was willing to do so herself, Sergeant Broderick felt it would cause more embarrassment for George to listen to his mother's explanation.

"Aye, I suppose you're right. I'll bring him down a cup of tea."

The job was almost complete by the time the sergeant carried the two cups of steaming hot liquid to where the young man stood, mopping his brow with his sleeve.

"You've broken out in a fine sweat there, son. Maybe I should have brought you some water instead."

"A cup of tea is very welcome, thank you, Sergeant. I'm almost done here," George glanced back at the house. "I've a game tomorrow but don't tell Nan."

"She knows you sneak off to play hurling but turns a blind eye to it nowadays. It's not easy for a mother to chastise her son when he's head and shoulders above her."

George laughed, "No, I don't suppose it is."

"Have you never been inclined to call her 'Ma' or 'Mother' seeing as she legally adopted you?" the sergeant asked.

"Not that I can remember. Nan never hid the truth about my adoption from me. I must have heard everyone else call her Mary-Anne and tried to do the same, only it came out more like 'Nan' and she liked the sound of it, I suppose."

"I like that name, too, but you're the only one she allows call her that. She did a fine job raising you those first few years of your life, it was one of the things that attracted me to her. She must have loved you very much to adopt you, son. We both do, you know that, don't you?"

The sergeant was leading up to the reason for bringing two cups of tea to the end of the garden. Noticing that George was beginning to shift uncomfortably on the low wall they were sitting on, he cleared his throat and got straight to the point.

"Your mother tells me you've been asking her a lot of questions lately about your father and who he might be."

The young man nodded his head and stared intently at the hens scratching about in the grass.

"Does the likeness between yourself and your cousin Tom have anything to do with your curiosity?" the sergeant asked.

George kept his eyes focused on the hens, "A person would have to be blind not to notice," he said.

"Did Tom say anything to you about it?"

"We never spoke of it, but I know it puzzled him. Especially after the telegram he received from his sister in New York. You know – the one about an inheritance from Doctor Gilmore," George thought for a moment then added, "Nan didn't save all that money to buy this house, did she, Sergeant?"

"No, son. She was paid to keep quiet. She even had to sign an agreement not to divulge who your father was."

"If Gilmore was my father does that mean Nan is really my mother? How else can I look so much like Tom?"

This was the question that Mary-Annc dreaded and had already discussed with her sister, Catherine. They agreed their sons would be told the truth, should they raise any questions about the uncanny resemblance the cousins bore to each other.

"It's a serious offence to forge a legal document and that's what your mother would have had to do to get another woman's name put on your birth certificate. Do you think she would do such a thing, lad?"

George shook his head.

"I'm going to share something with you that will explain the likeness between yourself and Tom. Your mother knows we are having this conversation, that's why we haven't heard a peep out of her. She's keeping well out of the way."

Sergeant Broderick went on to explain how Catherine came to be pregnant with Tom and that men of Gilmore's sort got away with such evil deeds because they knew they couldn't be touched.

George went very quiet and the sergeant allowed time for him to reflect upon the loathsome account he had just shared with him.

"My father wasn't a very nice man. I'm glad Nan took me away from him. Did you know he used to beat me for no reason at all?"

"I did, George. Your mother told me. She hoped you might have forgotten about your early years in his house. But you haven't, have you, lad?"

"His wife was always kind to me. Do you think she knew I was his son? How could she even stand the sight of me, knowing such a thing?"

The sergeant ruffled George's hair. "Because she was a good woman and knew that no blame could be laid on an innocent child."

More silence followed and the hens approached them to peck around their feet.

"So I have a half-brother. That's good news, for me at least. I like Tom, we got along very well and he's promised to keep in touch. But I feel sorry for what happened to Aunt Catherine," said George. "It's a terrible thing to be told your father was capable of such a vile act, one that he repeated God knows how many times."

"Now you know why your mother couldn't bring herself to tell you. I was reluctant to do it myself."

George rose quickly, startling the hens, and held out his hand.

"You've been like a father to me all these years. You're a decent man, Sergeant. A real decent man."

"Well now, you're not such a bad fellow yourself, George."

Mary-Anne was upstairs looking through the heavy lace curtains of a bedroom window and saw what took place at the end of her garden. The handshake told her the dreaded conversation had already taken place and she felt a stab of tears at the back of her eyes.

CHAPTER TWENTY-FIVE

Catherine raised her feet and placed them on the footstool between her armchair and Lily's. The apartment was so quiet the sounds from the street below seemed louder than usual.

"Have you a window open, Lily?"

"They're all open, are you cold, Catherine. Shall I close them?"

"I am, a wee bit. But no, leave the air get in."

The women discussed the mountain of sewing that had accumulated and congratulated themselves on having the foresight to have bought a second machine just before Catherine's trip back to Ireland.

"We'll catch up in no time, now that you're back," said Lily.

She noticed her sister-in-law shiver and closed the window in the parlour, in spite of Catherine's protests.

"Are you ailing?" Lily felt the other woman's forehead. "You don't seem to have a fever."

"It's the worry over Patrick that has me unwell. And how am I to face my son? Has he not told ye how much he inherited? What does a *'substantial amount'* mean?"

Lily shook her head, "I don't know. Thomas says it means a very large amount. I should never have told you about Patrick's visit the day he discovered what was in that letter. It was not my place to do so. But when he was the first person you asked about the minute you stepped foot off that ship, how could I lie to you?"

"I wouldn't want you to, Lily. At least now I'm prepared for whatever it is he shall say to me – or not say. He may never speak to me again, and who could blame him?"

Both women fell silent while they thought about Patrick's reaction to the revealing of such a long held dreadful secret. The thought of losing him made Catherine more aware of how much he meant to her, but she resolved in her heart to put up with whatever the consequences might be and to make the best of it.

"I cannot believe he is still capable of ruining my life," Catherine lamented.

"Who? Patrick?"

"No, Lily, not Patrick. Gilmore – that evil monster. Even in death he reaches out from the grave. His cruelty knows no boundaries."

"Is it possible his conscience bothered him? After all, he was gravely ill and, from what Tom has told us, it seems he changed his will not long before he died. He might have felt guilty for not providing for his son all these years. Or maybe he wanted to make amends for the hurt he caused you," suggested Lily.

Catherine shook her head vehemently, tears of rage spilling from her eyes.

"Make amends? Do you think he was ignorant of the hurt it would cause my husband, never mind myself? And what about Tom? No, Lily. Gilmore knew what he was doing. Mary-Anne told me he couldn't get rid of her and young George fast enough when his wife died. He paid her well for her silence, as long as she put enough distance between them."

"I don't know what to say, Catherine," Lily sighed. "Do you want me to go home with you? Jeremiah will be back from school soon."

"You're a good friend to me, Lily, and I thank you kindly for your offer. I shall be fine on my own," Catherine stood and brushed the creases from her skirt. "I should be setting off now if I'm to have a nice supper waiting for the family when they get home. The smell of good food at the end of a working day does wonders to lift the spirit, doesn't it, Lily?"

******

Ellen was the first to arrive, carrying a bundle of clothes she had been mending in her mother's absence. They were neatly folded but got crushed when Catherine tightly embraced her daughter.

"I take it you missed me, Ma, seeing as you're squeezing the life out of me. Mind the clothes, they'll be full of creases if you don't let go of me."

Catherine stood back, brushing a tear from her cheek, "Never mind the creases," she took the clothes from Ellen. "Stand back and let me look at you."

After her youngest had twirled and curtsied daintily, Catherine made her sit at the table while she poured them both some tea. Lily had already told her Ellen was living with them, so it was a surprise to hear she would be sleeping in her old room that night, with Maisie.

"It will be nice to catch up on what my sister is getting up to with that man of hers," Ellen had a mischievous glint in her eye. "But don't expect me to reveal any of her secrets to you, Ma. There's some things should never be shared with parents."

Catherine's heart almost stopped and she examined her daughter's face closely. Did Ellen already know the reason behind her brother's inheritance? Surely Lily would have warned her if that was the case. She did tell her that Patrick knew about Gilmore but never mentioned anything about her children finding out.

"Ma, sit down. I'll pour the tea, you've gone as white as a sheet. Are you ill?"

Shaking her head, Catherine took a seat at the table, realizing her daughter had spoken in a light-hearted manner. She inwardly scolded herself for reading more into Ellen's words than was there.

"It's all the traveling, love. I haven't slept very well these past few days. You know what I'm like on a ship."

Ellen accepted her mother's excuse and insisted on preparing the food for the evening meal.

"Don't worry, I shall let you make the sauce, Ma. The rest of them will know if I do it, and I'll never hear the end of their complaining. You make the finest bread sauce this side of the Atlantic, did you know that, Ma?"

The next hour passed with Ellen chatting away about anything and everything while her mother occasionally nodded her head, answering any questions with as few words as possible. Catherine tried not to look at the clock on the mantelpiece but every so often her daughter would catch her doing so and follow suit.

"Maisie will likely be home first, Ma? She's missed you something awful. I'll wager she runs up those stairs two steps at a time."

While both women were laughing at the image of Ellen's sister galloping up the stairs, she burst through the door and threw herself at Catherine. Whoops of joy and hugging and kissing went on for a good five minutes before another round of tea was poured and the trio settled around the table to share even more news.

It wasn't long before Tom was standing in the hallway outside his door. He could hear the sound of laughter and debated whether or not he should turn on his heel and walk back down the stairs. It was the thought of disappointing his mother that made him open the door and walk into the apartment.

Catherine was standing at the stove stirring a small pot while the girls chatted to her from the table. As soon as Tom walked into the room she ran towards him and knew the second she embraced him that something was wrong.

"Supper is ready, son. Your da shouldn't be too long, should he, Maisie?" Catherine turned to her daughter.

"Don't ask me, I'm only the foreman's lady-friend – not his boss," the sisters erupted into another round of laughter.

"Da said something at breakfast about going to a meeting this evening, so I suppose we should go ahead and eat without him," suggested Tom. "It could be midnight before he arrives home, Ma."

The young man was surprised to see a look of relief sweep over his mother's face. "I'll just have a quick wash before supper," he said.

CHAPTER TWENTY-SIX

The Gallagher family settled into an uneasy routine in the weeks following Catherine's return from Ireland. A heaviness of sorts hung in the air of what used to be a congenial and cheerful home. Opening the windows in every room gave access to the city breeze, which helped make the apartment seem light and airy, but it was mostly an illusion.

The day after she arrived in New York, Patrick demanded their children be told about Gilmore. A very subdued Catherine remained seated at the table with her family while her husband paced the length and breadth of the room, explaining the reason for Tom's large inheritance, word for word, as told to him by his wife. Even though he omitted to tell them about Gilmore forcing himself upon their mother, Catherine held her composure. The girls were astonished but could tell by Tom's expression the information wasn't new to him. As soon as they opened their mouths to question him, Patrick strode across the room to the door and left without saying another word.

Tom was torn between following his father, who was obviously very upset, and staying to give his mother the support she would need when filling in the gaps in the story for her daughters. When Catherine nodded towards the door, giving her son permission to leave, relief swept through the young man and he kissed her cheek, before leaving the apartment to chase after his father on the street below.

Since then, Catherine and Patrick could barely spend longer than fifteen minutes in each other's company before one of them would make an excuse to leave the room. Their children tried to give them space by arranging visits to friends on the same evening but their efforts had been in vain. The latest plan was to spend a night with Thomas and Lily, giving their parents the privacy to clear the air without fear of interruption.

Maisie and Tom had announced at breakfast one morning that they were going to a party with their sister Ellen, and would be staying over at their aunt and uncle's place. Patrick made no remark as he mopped up the remains of his egg with a slice of bread.

Their mother, on the other hand, smiled at both of them as she rose to clear the table. The siblings looked at the bowed head of their father and sighed. It would have been easy to blame him for the continued strain in the relationship, their mother seemed to be making more of an effort. Maisie had said as much to Tom as they parted company at the end of the block to go their separate ways to work. But he reminded her of the terrible secret that had recently been revealed to their father and of the pain it must have caused.

With the apartment to herself, Patrick having left soon after his children, Catherine tackled the rapidly shrinking pile of mending. It had been good to have something other than her fractured marriage to distract her. Holding up a sleeve she had just repaired, Catherine wished a needle and thread could do the same for the damage Gilmore had caused her family. Tom had taken everything in his stride and as far as anyone could tell, nothing had changed in his relationship with Patrick. In fact, father and son seemed to be closer than ever.

The hours passed by in a frenzy of sewing until there was nothing left to mend, except the hole in her Irish linen tablecloth. Catherine couldn't face threading one more needle and decided it would do her good to get out of the apartment. She would go in search of a nice piece of meat to make a special supper for when Patrick arrived home that evening.

As the day drew to a close, the sky darkened and the noise of the busy street below gradually diminished. Catherine resigned herself to the fact that Patrick was most likely waiting until she retired for the night before venturing home. She lit one of the two large kerosene lamps that hung on the wall each side of the chimney breast. Deciding on one last scan of the street below, Catherine stood by the parlour window, scrutinizing the shadowed entrance of the building opposite. Was Patrick standing in the darkness waiting for the light in the window to go out, before climbing the stairs to his apartment? Catherine poked her head through the open window and looked up towards the roof. A movement caught her eye and she quickly pulled herself back into the room.

That year, the early summer weather had been extremely warm and when the really hot nights arrived people would be dragging their mattresses to the roofs of their buildings to sleep under the stars, in an attempt to cool down. Throughout the city the rooftops and fire escapes would be covered in sleeping tenants, grateful for the night-time drop in temperature. Even in cooler weather, the roof was always a favourite haunt of Patrick's, especially when the children were younger and noisier but it had been a few years since he felt the need to escape from his family – until now.

Catherine was unable to eat the food she had prepared that evening and had been keeping it warm between two plates, set over a pot of simmering water. She unpegged a towel from the line over the stove and wrapped it around the plates, before carrying them from the apartment to the top floor of their building. A rough wooden stairs had been put in place to allow access to the rooftop and Catherine steadied herself against the wall while balancing the hot plates as she climbed.

The narrow sloped door on the hatch at the top of the stairs was closed. As she pushed it open her heart raced with anxiety as to what kind of a reception she would receive, should Patrick be there. For a moment, just before stepping out onto the roof, Catherine almost hoped she would find herself alone.

"Patrick," she listened for a reply. "Patrick, are you up here?"

Still no response, the only sound coming from the streets far below. Across the roof stood large chimney stacks and the smell of

162

coal fires, banked down for the night in their stoves, hung in the air.

Catherine stood very still in the darkness and held out the plates, still wrapped in the towel.

"I brought you up your supper," her voice wavered. "I can leave it here and go back down. Please call out and at least let me know that you've heard me. I'm worried sick about you, love, but I'll leave you in peace – if that's what you want."

Catherine bent low and placed the meal on an upturned crate lying nearby, then turned back towards the stairs as she raised herself. Thinking she had made a big mistake in coming up onto the rooftop, she was beginning to feel foolish. What if Patrick wasn't even there? What if it was a stranger she had seen from her window? Someone who might be lurking in the shadows, waiting to attack her at any moment?

Very quickly, Catherine's feeling of embarrassment turned to one of fear. In her haste to get to the open hatch she stumbled and cried out as a dark figure rushed out from behind one of the chimney stacks towards her.

Patrick's voice cut through the panic that had Catherine almost on the verge of screaming. By the time he reached her she was on her knees, her face buried in her hands.

"Are you alright, Catherine," his words calmed her immediately.

"I got such a fright. The thought suddenly occurred to me that it might not be you up here after all."

Before Patrick could take a step nearer, Catherine was on her feet, brushing the dust from the roof off her skirt. She was thankful for the thickly clouded sky blotting out the moon and stars. The lights of the city were also dim enough to shade their faces and, unable to read his expression even from the few feet between them, she turned away from Patrick.

"I'd best leave you to get on with your meal before it gets any colder."

Just as she was about to put a foot through the hatch Patrick called out to her.

"I suppose you've already eaten, have you?" he asked.

Catherine did not turn around but shook her head, "No. I was waiting until you came home."

As he picked up the plates he felt the weight in them and offered to share the meal with her if she was hungry, "This feels heavy enough to feed a family. I doubt I would manage to eat it all at this late hour."

The seconds dragged silently by.

"It would be a shame to waste good food, Catherine."

When his wife turned around to face him, Patrick moved a few steps closer. He held out his hand and offered to guide her across the roof to one of the chimney stacks. It was the first time they had touched each other in months.

"Step into my parlour," he gestured with the plate of food, unwilling to let go of her hand.

Upturned wooden crates, similar to the one she had placed his meal on, were lined against the brick stack. Catherine sat down on a hay-filled sack that she guessed Patrick had been using as a mattress, whenever he disappeared in the middle of the night. He had taken to waiting for half an hour after his wife had gone to bed before retiring himself, and always lay with his back towards her.

Since her return from Ireland, Catherine had reached out to Patrick every night but each time his response was the same – to move away to the edge of their bed or leave it altogether. Some mornings she would find him asleep in his armchair by the stove, and wondered how he could do a full day's labouring with the stiffness it must have caused in his back.

"I forgot to bring up the cutlery, Patrick. Shall I go back down and fetch it?"

This was a good excuse to release her husband's hand, neither of them wanting to be the first one to let go. Patrick sat down beside Catherine and shook his head.

"There's no need to, I can eat with my hands. It won't be the first time," he unwrapped the towel and held out one of the plates. "You can't let me eat this fine meal alone, now, can you?"

It wasn't just their empty stomachs that were filled by that shared meal. As they ate in silence they both felt the space between them grow smaller and an old familiar contentment settle over them. Words of explanation and forgiveness would come later, along with tears, but at that moment in time, a quiet healing had begun.

In contemplative silence, the plates were cleared of food and placed on a crate next to a jar containing a flickering candle. The couple moved closer to each other and looked out over the city, still absorbed in their own thoughts. They had been sitting holding hands without uttering a word for the best part of an hour, when Catherine felt a shiver go through her. Patrick put an arm around her and suggested they go down to their bed and put some heat back into their bodies. He wasn't sure if his wife understood his meaning but hoped that she did.

"It's true then, what Aunt Maggie always says," said Catherine.

"Your aunt comes out with a lot of strange sayings," Patrick teased. "Which of them are you referring to?"

Catherine picked up the jar and held it high, her face illuminated in the candlelight. She looked directly at her husband, hoping he would see the glint in her eye.

"That the way to a man's heart is through his belly."

THE END

(Book 7 to follow)

REFERENCES

Chapter Eight

Jacob Riis (1849-1914)

Riis emigrated from Denmark to America in 1870. He became a police reporter and used his camera to highlight the hardships of the tenements and became known as an advocate of social reform. His book *How the Other Half Lives* included the photographs he took of those who lived in the slums of New York and it helped to raise awareness of the need for change.

Chapter Eleven

1893 Crisis

The financial depression that occurred in that year in the United States was the worst in the history of the nation up to that point in time. It lasted for another four years. Panic stricken investors sold off assets, converting them into gold and the Treasury's reserves fell drastically. Banks called in loans but many of them still failed. Little was done by government to help those finding themselves out of work due to the many business that went under – there was no social welfare system in place at the time. 1894 almost two and a half million men went from city to city looking for work of any kind. Those lucky enough to have a job suffered steep pay cuts which led to strikes across the country. About 750,000 workers employed in factories and mines went on strike in 1894.

http://www.encyclopedia.com/history/united-states-and-canada/us-history/panic-1893

Chapter Sixteen

Mulberry Street.

From the 1890's Mulberry Street was mostly populated by immigrants from Italy and was described as the Main Street of Little Italy. In 1888 the Tenement House Committee of New York drew up plans for Mulberry Park which made up the tenement area known as 'The Bend'. However, it took six more years for the dilapidated properties in that area to be bought up. The delay was mainly due to city officials hesitating to interfere with the landlords.

https://historyengine.richmond.edu/episodes/view/4476

Chapter 20

£500 in 1885 would equal approx. £49,000 or $63,000 in 2016.

Uisce beatha (water of life) – the Irish word for whiskey.

Chapter 22

Scurvyworth.

So called because its leaves contain vitamin C. This little perennial plant is one of the first to flower in late winter, blooming in hedgerows and woodland, and by rivers and roadsides, between February and May. William Wordsworth even penned a poem about it;

'There is a Flower, the Lesser Celandine,
That shrinks, like many more, from cold and rain;
And, at the first moment that the sun may shine,
Bright as the sun itself, 'tis out again!'

From *The Small Celandine.*

AUTHOR BIO

Jean Reinhardt was born in Louth, grew up in Dublin and lived in Alicante, Spain for almost eight years. With five children and three grandchildren, life is never dull. She now lives in Ireland and loves to read, write, listen to music and spend time with family and friends. When Jean isn't writing she likes to take long walks through the woods and on the beach.

Jean writes poetry, short stories and novels. Her favourite genres are Young Adult and Historical Fiction. She loves to hear from readers and can be contacted on the following sites:

Website:
www.jeanreinhardt.wordpress.com

Facebook:
www.facebook.com/JeanReinhardtWriter

Twitter:
www.twitter.com/JeanReinhardt1

ACKNOWLEDGEMENTS

A great big thank you to beta readers, Anne, Joyce, Ken, Ellen, Patricia, Peter, Brenda, Jennifer, Ann, Carol Eileen and to Motoko for suggesting the Family Tree.

The following books proved to be a great source of information in the writing of this story. They are full of well documented events and photographs of people whose families have lived in Blackrock for many generations, including my own:

The Parish of Haggardstown & Blackrock – A History by Noel Sharkey.
First Printed in 2003 by Dundalgan Press (W. Tempest) Ltd., Dundalk.

The Parish of Haggardstown & Blackrock – A Pictorial Record
Compiled and written by Noel Sharkey with photos by Owen Byrne.
Printed in 2008 by Dundalgan Press (W. Tempest) Ltd., Dundalk.

Made in United States
North Haven, CT
13 November 2021

11128391R00102